William Boyd

On the Yankee Station

William Boyd's first novel, *A Good Man in Africa*, won a Whitbread Prize and a Somerset Maugham Award; his second, *An Ice-Cream War*, was awarded the John Llewellyn Rhys Prize and was shortlisted for the Booker Prize. *Brazzaville Beach* won the James Tait Memorial Prize and *The Blue Afternoon* won the Los Angeles Times Prize for Fiction. Boyd lives in London.

INTERNATIONAL

On the Yankee Station

On the Yankee Station

Stories

William Boyd

VINTAGE INTERNATIONAL
Vintage Books
A Division of Random House, Inc.
New York

FIRST VINTAGE INTERNATIONAL EDITION, FEBRUARY 2001

Copyright © 1981, 1982 by William Boyd

Some of these stories have appeared in the following: *London Magazine, Mayfair, Punch, Isis, The Literary Review*, BBC Radio 4's *Morning Story, Company*, and *New Stories 6*.

Library of Congress Cataloging-in-Publication Data
Boyd, William, 1952–
On the Yankee station : stories / by William Boyd.
p. cm.
ISBN: 0-375-70511-2
I. Title
PR6052.O9192 O5 2001
823'.914—dc21
00-063409

Author photograph © Jerry Bauer

www.vintagebooks.com

Printed in the United States of America
10 9 8 7 6 5 4 3 2 1

For Susan

Contents

On the Yankee Station

Next Boat from Douala

Then the brothel was raided. Christ, he'd only gone down to Spinoza's to confront Patience with her handiwork. She hadn't been free when Morgan first arrived, so he had chatted to the owner, Baruch—as his better-read clients whimsically dubbed the diminutive Levantine pimp—for half an hour or so, and watched the girls dancing listlessly under the roof fans. His anger had subsided a bit but he managed to stoke up a rage when he was eventually ushered into Patience's cubicle. "Hey!" he had roared, lowering his greyish Y-fronts. "Bloody look at this mess!" But then his tirade had been cut short by the whistles and stompings of Sgt. Mbele and his vice squad.

The day had started badly. Morgan woke, hot and sweaty, his sheets damp binding-cloths. Three things presented themselves to his mind almost simultaneously: it was Christmas Eve, in four days he would be catching the next boat home from Douala and he had a dull ache in his groin. He eased his seventeen-and-a-half stone out of bed and started for the bathroom. There, a hesitant diagnosis set off by the unfamiliar pain was horrifyingly confirmed by the sight of his opaque, forked and pustular urine.

He dropped off at the local clinic before going in to

the office. Inside it was cool and air-conditioned. Outside, in the shade cast by the wide eaves, mothers and children sprawled. And inside he ruefully confessed to a Calvinistic Scottish doctor, young and unrelentingly professional, of his weekly visits to Patience at Spinoza's. Then a plump black sister led him to an ante-room where, retreating coyly behind a screen, he delivered up a urine sample. The clear tinkle of his stream on the thin glass of the bottle seemed to rebound deafeningly from the tiled walls. With a cursoriness teetering on the edge of contempt, the doctor told him that the result of the test would be available tomorrow.

He vented his embarrassment and mounting anger at his office, Nkongsamba's Deputy High Commission, turning down all that day's applications for visas out of hand, vetoing the recommendations of senior missionaries for candidates in the next birthday honours and, exquisite zenith of the day's attack of spleen, peremptorily sacking a filing clerk for eating fu-fu while handling correspondence. He began to feel a little better, the fear of some hideous social disease retreating as time interposed itself between now and his visit to the clinic.

After lunch his air-conditioner broke down. Morgan detested the sun, and because of his corpulence his three years in Nkongsamba had been three years of seemingly constant perspiration, virulent rashes and general discomfort. He had accepted the posting gladly, proud to tell family and friends he was in the Diplomatic Service, and had enthusiastically read the literature of West Africa, searching, with increasing despair, first in Joyce Cary, then through Graham Greene, right down to Gerald Durrell and Conrad, for any experience that vaguely corresponded with his own. When the cream tropical suit he had so keenly bought began to grow mould in the armpits—a creeping greenish hue eventually encroaching on the button-down flap of a breast pocket—he had forthwith abandoned it, and with it all hopes of injecting a literary frisson into his dull and routine life. But, thank God, he was leaving it all soon, next boat from Douala, leaving the steaming forest, the truculent natives, the tiny black flies that raised florin-sized bites. What would he miss? The beer, strong and cold, and of course Patience, with her lordotic posture, pragmatic sex, and her smooth black body smelling strangely of "Amby," a skin-lightening agent that sold very well in these parts.

Morgan came home after work. There had been an unexpected fall of rain during the afternoon. The air was heavy and damp; great ranges of purple cumulus loomed in the sky. He climbed up the steps to his stoop, shouting for Pious, his houseboy, to bring beer. There on the stoop table lay his copy of Keats, sole heritage of his years at his plate-glass university. He had come across it while packing and had glanced through it, with nostalgic affection, at breakfast. Now, carelessly left out in the rain, it sat there swollen, and steaming slightly, it seemed, in the late-afternoon heat—a grotesque papier-mâché brick. He picked it up and bellowed for Pious.

He stood under the cold shower, allowing the stream of water to course down his face, plastering his thinning hair to his forehead. A startled Pious had received the sodden complete works full in the face and when he scrabbled to pick it up, Morgan had booted him viciously in the arse. He smiled, then frowned. The sudden movement, though producing a satisfying yelp from Pious, had done some damage. Pain pulsed like a Belisha beacon from his testicles, now, he was convinced, grown palpably larger. He counted slowly from one to ten. Things were ganging up on him; he was beginning to feel insecure, hunted almost. Only three days to the boat, then away, thank Christ, for good.

They became very friendly, more by force of circum-
stance—they were both alone, unattractive and need-
ing to forget it—than by desire. At midnight they kissed
and she stuck her tongue in his ear. There was no sign
of Brian. Morgan remembered them now from the
cocktail party at the Commission. Brinkit small, bald and
shy. Doreen six inches taller than he. Brinkit telling him
of his desire to leave Africa and become a vet in Devon.
Wanted kids, nothing quite like family life. No place for
children, Africa—very risky, health-wise. No place for
you either, Morgan had thought, as he looked at the
man's little eyes and his frail, earnest features.

Some time later in a dark corner of the ballroom Doreen squirmed and hissed, "No! Morgan! Stop it . . .
honestly, not *here*." Then more suggestively: "Look, why
don't I give you a run home. I've got the van outside."

Breathless with excitement and lust, Morgan excused
himself for a moment. On his way to the lavatory he
reflected that possibly it hadn't been such a bad day after
all. God. A real white woman.

But then a five-minute session of searing agony in the
gent's toilet brought home to him—with an awful clarity—the nightmarish significance of the lyrics in Jerry
Lee Lewis' "Great Balls of Fire." He reeled out of the
toilet, eyes streaming, teeth clenched, and collided with
a small, firm object. Through the mists of tears, the prim
features of his doctor shimmered and formed, mouth
like a recently sutured wound.

"Oh! Morgan, it's you. Well, I won't waste any words.
Save you a trip tomorrow. Bad news, I'm afraid. You've
got gonorrhoea." As if he didn't know.

The VW bus was parked up a track off the main road
some miles out of town. The jungle reared up on all
sides. Heavy rain beat down remorselessly. Inside, lit by

the inadequate glow of a map light, Morgan and Doreen Brinkit lay in the back, spacious with the seats folded down. Doreen moaned unconvincingly as Morgan nuzzled her neck. His heart wasn't in it. His mind was obsessed with a single image, rooted there since he'd heard the appalling news, of a rancid gherkin astride two suppurating black olives. With a shudder he broke off and took great pulls at the gin bottle he'd purchased before leaving the club. His brain seemed to cartwheel crazily in his skull. Bloody country! he screamed inwardly. Bloody filthy Patience! Three rotting years just to end up with the clap. He drank deep, awash with self-pity. A tense, frustrated rage mounted within him. Distractedly he looked round. Doreen was tugging at the bodice of her dress, all tulle and taffeta, reinforced with bakelite and whalebone. She pulled it down, revealing an absurd cut-away bra that offered her nipples like canapés on a cocktail tray. Morgan's rage was replaced by a spasm of equally intense lust. What the hell, he was on the next boat from Douala, clearing out. She was desperate for it. He reached up and switched out the map light.

But then somewhere in the prolonged pre-coital tussle, with Doreen's dress concertina-ed at her waist, Morgan's trousers at his knees, the rain drumming on the tin roof, the air soupy with sweat and deep breathing, Morgan took stock. Perhaps it was when she breathed, "Come on, Morgan, it's okay, it's okay. It's the safe time of the month," and Morgan, spliced between Doreen's pale shanks, looked up at the windscreen awash with water, and images began to zigzag through his mind like bats in a room seeking an open window. He thought of his testicles effervescing with bacilli; he thought of pathetic Brian Brinkit searching for his fucking dachshund in a downpour; then he thought of impregnating

Doreen, his putrid seed in her womb, Brian's innocent
alarm at the diseased monster he'd inadvertently produced. He thought of Brian diseased, too, a loathsome
spiral of infection, a little septic carbuncle festering in
Africa behind him. And he realised as Doreen's grunts
began to reach a crescendo beneath him that, no, in spite
of everything—Patience, Keats, Pious, Mbele, the stinking heat and the clap—it just wasn't on.

He withdrew and sat up, breathing heavily.

"What is it, Morgan?" Surprised, a tint of anger col-
ouring her voice.

What the hell could he say? "I'm sorry, Doreen," he
began pathetically, desperately running through plau-
sible reasons. "But . . . it's just, um . . . well, I don't
think this is fair to Brian. I mean . . . he is out looking
for Tom, in this rain." Then, despite himself, he
laughed, a half-suppressed derisive snort, and Doreen
abruptly burst into tears, sobbing as she tried to cover
herself up. Morgan sat and finished the gin.

"*Get out!*" Morgan looked round in alarm. Doreen, hair
all over the place, face tracked with mascara, shrieking
at him. "Fucking get *out*! How *dare* you treat me like
this! You filth, you fat sodding bastard!" She started to
pummel him with her fists, pushing him towards the
back of the van with surprising strength. Somehow the
door sprang open.

"Hang on, Doreen! It's pouring. Let's talk about it."
She was hitting him about the head and shoulders with
the empty gin bottle, screaming obscenities all the while.
Morgan fell out of the back of the van. He scampered
out of the way seconds later as she reversed violently
down the road. Morgan sat on the verge, the jungle at
his back, rain soaking him completely. "Jesus," he said.
He wiped his wet hair from his forehead. For some curious reason he felt light-headed, suddenly hugely re-

lieved. He got to his feet noticing unconcernedly that his trousers were covered in mud. Then, for a brief tranquil moment, the rain beating down on his head, he felt intensely, exhilaratingly happy. Why? He couldn't really be sure. Still . . . He set off down the track, a bulky, dripping figure, humming quietly to himself at first and then, spontaneously, filling his lungs and breaking into a booming cockney basso profundo that spilled out into the dark and over the trees.

"Hyme a si-i-inging in a ryne, hyme a singin' in a ryne."

Cicadas trilled in his path.

Not Yet, Jayette

This happened to me in L.A. once. Honestly. I was standing at a hamburger kiosk on Echo Park eating a chili dog. This guy in a dark green Lincoln pulls up at the curb in front of me and leans out the window. "Hey," he asks me, "do you know the way to San José?" Well, that threw me, I had to admit it. In fact I almost told him. Then I got wise. "Don't tell me," I says. "Let me guess. You're going back to find some peace of mind." I only tell you this to give you some idea of what the city is like. It's full of jokers. And that guy, even though I'd figured him, still bad-mouthed me before he drove away. That's the kind of place it is. I'm just telling you so's you know my day is for real.

Most mornings, early, I go down to the beach at Santa Monica to try and meet Christopher Isherwood. A guy I know told me he likes to walk his dog down there before the beach freaks and the surfers show up. I haven't seen him yet but I've grown to like my mornings on the beach. The sea has that oily sheen to it, like an empty swimming pool. The funny thing is, though, the Pacific Ocean nearly always looks cold. One morning someone was swinging on the bars, up and down, flinging himself about as if he was made of rubber. It was beautiful, and boy, was he built. It's wonderful to me what the human body can achieve if you treat it right. I like to keep in shape. I work out. So most days I hang around waiting to see if Christopher's going to show. Then I go jogging. I head south, down from the pier to Pacific Ocean Park. I've got to know some of the bums that live around the beach, the junkies and derelicts. "Hi, Charlie," they shout when they see me jogging by.

There's a café in Venice where I eat breakfast. A girl works there most mornings, thin, bottle-blond, kind of tired-looking. I'm pretty sure she's on something heavy. So that doesn't make her anything special but she can't be more than eighteen. She knows my name—I don't know how. I never told her. Anyway, each morning when she brings me my coffee and doughnut she says, "Hi there, Charlie. Lucked out yet?

I just smile and say, "Not yet, Jayette." Jayette's the name she's got sewn across her left tit. I'm not sure I like the way she speaks to me—I don't exactly know what she's referring to. But seeing how she knows my name I think it must be my career she's talking about. Because I used to be a star—well, a TV star anyway. Between the ages of nine and eleven I earned $12,000 a week. Perhaps you remember the show, a TV soap opera called *The Scrantons*. I was the little brother, Chuck. For two years I was a star. I got the whole treatment: my own trailer, chauffeured limousines, private tutors. Trouble was my puberty came too early. Suddenly I was like a teenage gatecrasher at a kids' party. My voice went, I got zits all over my chin, fluff on my lip. It spoiled everything. Within a month the scenario for my contractual death was drawn up. I think it was pneumonia, or maybe an accident with the thresher. I can't really remember; I don't like to look back on those final days.

Though I must confess it was fun meeting all the stars. The big ones: Jeanne Lamont, Eddy Cornelle, Mary and

Marvin Keen—you remember them. One of the most
bizarre features of my life since I left the studio is that
nowadays I never see stars anymore. Isn't that ridiculous? Someone like me who worked with them, who
practically lives in Hollywood? Somehow I never get to
see the stars anymore. I just miss them. "Oh, he left five
minutes ago, bub," or, "Oh, no, I think she's on loca-
tion in Europe. She hasn't been here for weeks." The
same old story.

I think that's what Jayette's referring to when she asks
if I've lucked out. She knows I'm still hanging in there,
waiting. I mean, I've kept on my agent. The way I see
it is that once you've been in front of the cameras,
something's going to keep driving you on until you get
back. I know it'll happen to me again one day. I just
have this feeling inside.

After breakfast I jog back up the beach to where I
left the car. One morning I got to thinking about Jayette. What does she think when she sees me now and
remembers me from the days of *The Scrantons*? It seems
to me that everybody in their life is at least two people.
Once when you're a child and once when you're an
adult. It's the saddest thing. I don't just mean that you
see things differently when you're a child—that's something else again. What's sad is that you can't seem to
keep the personality. I know I'm not the same person
anymore as young Chuck Scranton was, and I find that
depressing. I could meet little Charlie on the beach today and say, "Look, there goes a sharp kid." And never
recognize him, if you see what I mean. It's a shame.

I don't like the jog back so much, as all the people
are coming out. Lying around, surfing, cruising, scor-
ing, shooting up, tricking. Hell, the things I've seen on
that sand, I could tell you a few stories. Sometimes I
like to go down to El Segundo or Redondo Beach just
to feel normal.

I usually park the car on Santa Monica Palisades. I
tidy up, change into my clothes and shave. I have a small
battery-powered electric razor that I use. Then I have
a beer, wander around, buy a newspaper. Mostly I then
drive north to Malibu. There's a place I know where
you can get a fair view of a longish stretch of the beach.
It's almost impossible to get down there in summer; they
don't like strangers. So I pull off the highway and climb
this small dune hill. I have a pair of opera glasses of
my aunt's that I use to see better—my eyesight's not too
hot. I spotted Rod Steiger one day, and Jane Fonda I
think but I can't be sure; the glasses tend to fuzz everything a bit over four hundred yards. Anyway, I like the
quiet on that dune. It's restful.

I have been down onto Malibu Beach, but only in the
winter season. The houses are all shut up but you can
still get the feel of it. Some people were having a barbecue one day. It looked good. They had a fire going
on a big porch that jutted out high over the sand. They
waved and shouted when I went past.

Lunch is bad. The worst part of the day for me because I have to go home. I live with my aunt. I call her
my aunt though I'm not related to her at all. She was
my mother's companion—I believe that's the right
word—until my mother stuffed her face with a gross of
Seconal one afternoon in a motel at Corona del Mar. I
was fifteen then and Vanessa—my "aunt"—became some
kind of legal guardian to me and had control of all the
money I'd made from *The Scrantons*. Well, she bought
an apartment in Beverly Glen because she liked the address. Man, was she swallowed by the realtor. They build
these tiny apartment blocks on cliff-faces up the asshole of the big-name canyons just so you can say you
live off Mulholland Drive or in Bel-Air. It's a load. I'd
rather live in Watts or on Imperial Highway. I practically have to rope up and wear crampons to get to my

front door. And it is mine. I paid for it.

Maybe that's why Vanessa never leaves her bed. It's just too much effort getting in and out of the house. She just stays in bed all day and eats, watches TV and feeds her two dogs. I only go in there for lunch; it's my only "family" ritual. I take a glass of milk and a salad sandwich but she phones out for pizza and enchiladas and burgers—any kind of crap she can smear over her face and down her front. She's really grown fat in the ten years since my mother bombed out. But she still sits up in bed with those hairy yipping dogs under her armpits, and she's got her top and bottom false eyelashes, her hairpiece and purple lipstick on. I say nothing usually. For someone who never gets out she sure can talk a lot. She wears these tacky satin and lace peignoirs, shows half her chest. Her breasts look like a couple of Indian clubs rolling around under the shimmer. It's unfair, I suppose, but when I drive back into the foothills I like to think I'm going to have a luncheon date with . . . with someone like Grace Kelly—as was— or maybe Alexis Smith. I don't know. I wouldn't mind a meal and a civilized conversation with some nice people like that. But lunch with Vanessa? Thanks for nothing, pal. God, you can keep it. She's a real klutz. I'm sure Grace and Alexis would never let themselves get that way—you know, like Vanessa's always dropping tacos down her cleavage or smearing mustard on her chins.

I always get depressed after lunch. It figures, I hear you say. I go to my room and sometimes I have a drink (I don't smoke, so dope's out). Other days I play my guitar or else work on my screenplay. It's called *Walk. Don't Walk.* I get a lot of good ideas after lunch for some reason. That's when I got the idea for my screenplay. It just came to me. I remembered how I'd been stuck

one day at the corner of Arteria Boulevard and Nor-
mandie Avenue. There was a pile of traffic and the pe-
destrian signs were going berserk. "Walk" would come
on, so I'd start across. Two seconds later, "Don't Walk,"
so I go back. Then on comes "Walk" again. This went
on for ten minutes: "Walk. Don't Walk. Walk. Don't
Walk." I was practically out of my box. But what really
stunned me was the way I just stayed there and obeyed
the goddam machine for so long—I never even thought
about going it alone. Then one afternoon after lunch
it came to me that it was a neat image for life; just the
right kind of metaphor for the whole can of worms. The
final scene of this movie is going to be a slow crane shot
away from this malfunctioning traffic sign going "Walk.
Don't Walk." Then the camera pulls farther up and away
in a helicopter and you see that in fact the whole city is
fouled up because of this one sign flashing. They don't
know what to do; the programming's gone wrong. It's
a great final scene. Only problem is I'm having some
difficulty writing my way toward it. Still, it'll come, I
guess.

   In the late afternoon I go to work. I work at the Beverly Hills Hotel. Vanessa's brother-in-law got me the job.
I park cars. I keep hoping I'm going to park the car
of someone really important. Frank—that's Vanessa's
brother-in-law—will say to me, "Give this one a shine-
up, Charlie. It belongs to so-and-so. He produced this
film." Or, "That guy's the money behind X's new movie."
Or, "Look out, he's Senior Vice-President of Something Incorporated." I say, big deal. These guys hand
me the keys—they all look like bank clerks. If that's the
movies nowadays I'm not so sure I want back in.

   Afternoons are quiet at the hotel so I catch up on my
reading. I'm reading Camus at the moment but I think
I've learned all I can from him so I'm going on to Jung.

I don't know too much about Jung but I'm told he was really into astrology, which has always been a pet interest of mine. One thing I will say for quitting the movies when I did—it means I didn't miss out on my education. I hear that some of these stars today are really dumb; you know, they've got their brains in their neck and points south.

After work I drive back down to the Santa Monica Pier and think about what I'm going to do all night. The Santa Monica Pier is a kind of special place for me: it's the last place I saw my wife and son. I got married at seventeen and was divorced by twenty-two, though we were apart for a couple of years before that. Her name was Harriet. It was okay for a while but I don't think she liked Vanessa. Anyway, get this. She left me for a guy who was the assistant manager in the credit collection department of a large mail-order firm. I couldn't believe it when she told me. I said to her when she moved out that it had to be the world's most boring job and did she know what she was getting into? I mean, what sort of person do you have to be to take on that kind of work? The bad thing was she took my son, Skiff, with her. It's a dumb name, I know, but at the time he was born all the kids were being called things like Sky and Saffron and Powie, and I was really sold on sailing. I hope he doesn't hold it against me.

The divorce was messy and she got custody, though I'll never understand why. She had left some clothes at the house and wanted them back so she suggested we meet at the end of the Santa Monica Pier for some reason. I didn't mind—it was the impetuous side to her nature that first attracted me. I handed the clothes over. She was a bit tense. Skiff was running about; he didn't seem to know who I was. She was smoking a lot, those long-thin menthol cigarettes. I really didn't say anything much at all, asked her how she was, what school Skiff was going to. Then she just burst out: "Take a good look, Charlie. Then don't come near us ever again!" Her exact words. Then they went away.

So I go down to the end of the pier most nights and look out at the ocean and count the planes going in to land at L.A. International and try to work things out. Just the other evening I wandered up the beach a way and this thin-faced man with short gray hair came up to me and said, "Jordan, is that you?" And when he saw he'd made a mistake he smiled a nice smile, apologized and walked off. It was only this morning that I thought it might have been Christopher Isherwood himself. The more I think about it, the more convinced I become. What a perfect opportunity and I had to go and miss it. As I say: "Walk. Don't Walk." That's the bottom line.

I suppose I must have been preoccupied. The pier brings back all these memories like some private video loop, and my head gets to feel like it's full of birds all flapping around trying to get out. And also things haven't been so good lately. On Friday, Frank told me not to bother showing up at the hotel next week, I can't seem to make any headway with the screenplay, and for the last three nights Vanessa's tried to climb into my bed.

Well, tonight I think I'll drive to this small bar I know on Sunset. Nothing too great, a little dark. They do a nice white wine with peach slices in it, and there's some topless, some go-go, and I hear tell that Bobby De Niro sometimes shows up for a drink.

Hardly Ever

"Think of it," Holland said. "The sex."

"Sex," Panton repeated. "God . . . sex."

Niles shook his head. "Are you sure?" he asked. "I mean, can you guarantee it? The sex, that is. I don't want to waste time farting around singing."

"Waste bloody time? Are you mad?" Holland said. "It only happens every two years. You can't afford to miss the opportunity. Unless you're suffering from second thoughts."

"What, *me*?" Niles tried to laugh. He looked at Holland's blue eyes. They always seemed to know. "You must be bloody kidding, mate. Jesus, if you think . . . God!" he snorted.

"All right, all right," Holland said. "We agreed, remember? It's got to be all of us."

Niles had never asked for this last fact to be explained. Why, if—as Holland attested—the sex was freely available, on a plate so to speak, why did they all have to participate at the feast? Holland made out it was part of his naturally generous personality. It was more fun if you all had a go.

"Let's get on with it," Panton said.

They walked over to the notice-board. Holland pushed some juniors out of the way. Prothero, the music master, had written at the top of a sheet of paper: GILBERT

AND SULLIVAN OPERA — HMS PINAFORE — CHORUS: BASSES AND TENORS WANTED. SIGN BELOW. Half a dozen names had been scrawled down.

"Cretins," Holland said. "No competition." He wrote his name down. Panton followed suit.

Niles took a Biro from his blazer pocket. He paused. "But how can you be so sure? That's what I want to know. How can you tell that the girls just won't be— well—music lovers?"

"Because I know," Holland said patiently. "Every Gilbert and Sullivan it's the same. Borthwick told me. He was in the last one. He said the girls only come for one thing. I mean, it stands to reason. What sort of girl's going to want to be in some pissing bloody operetta. Ask yourself. Shitty orchestra, home-made costumes, people who can't sing to save their life. I tell you, Nilo, they're doing it for the same reason as us. They're fed up with the local yobs. They want a nice public school boy. Christ, you must have heard. It's a cert. Leave it to Pete."

Niles screwed up his eyes. What the hell, he thought, it's time I tried. He signed his name: Q. Niles.

"Good old Quentin," Panton roared. "Wor! Think of it waiting." He forced his features into a semblance of noble suffering, wrapped his arms around himself as if riven with acute internal pain and lurched drunkenly about, groaning in simulated ecstasy.

Holland grabbed Niles by the arm. "The shafting, Nilo, my man," he said intensely. "The royal bloody shafting we're going to do."

Niles felt his chest expand with sudden exhilaration. Holland's fierce enthusiasm always affected him more than Panton's most baroque histrionics.

"Bloody right, Pete," he said. "Too bloody right. I'm getting desperate already."

***

Niles sat in his small box-like study and stared out at the relentless rain falling on the gentle Scottish hills. From his study window he could see a corner of the dormitory wing of his own house, an expanse of gravel with the housemaster's car parked on it, and fifty yards of the drive leading down to the main school house a mile or so away. On the desk in front of him lay a half-completed team list for the inter-house rugby leagues and an open note pad. On the note pad he had written: " 'The Rape of the Lock,' " and below that, " 'The Rape of the Lock' is a mock heroic poem. What do you understand by this term? Illustrate with examples." It was an essay he was due to hand in tomorrow. He had no idea what to say. He gazed dully out at the rain, idly noting some boys coming out of the woods. They must be desperate, he thought, if they have to go out for a smoke in this weather. He returned to his more immediate problem. Who was going to play scrum-half now that Damianos had a sick-chit? He considered the pool of players he could draw on: asthmatics, fatsos, spastics every one. To hell with it. He wrote down Grover's name. They had no chance of winning anyway. He opened his desk cupboard and removed a packet of Jaffa cakes and a large bottle of Coca-Cola. He gulped thirstily from the bottle and ate a few biscuits. "The Rape of the Lock." What could he say about it? He didn't mind the poem. He thought of Belinda:

"On her white breast a sparkling cross she wore, . . ."
He found her far and away the most alluring of the fictional heroines he had yet encountered in his brief acquaintance with English Literature. He read the opening of the poem again. He saw her lying in a huge rumpled bed, a lace peignoir barely covering two breasts as firm and symmetrical as halved grapefruits. He had

had a bonk-on all the English lesson. It hadn't happened to him since they'd read *Great Expectations*. What
was her name? Estella. God, yes. She was almost as good
as Belinda. He thought about his essay again. He liked
English Literature. He wondered if he would be able to
do it at university—if he could get to university at all.
His father had not been at all pleased when he had announced that he wanted to do English A-level. "What's
the use of that?" he had shouted. "How's English Literature going to help you sell machine tools?" Niles
sighed. There was an opening for him in Gerald Niles
(Engineering) Ltd. His father knew nothing of his plans
for university.

Niles ran his hands through his thick wiry hair and
rubbed his eyes. He picked up his pen. "Alexander
Pope," he wrote, "was a major poet of the Augustan
period. 'The Rape of the Lock' was his most celebrated
poem." He sensed it was a bad beginning—uninspired,
boring—but sometimes if you started by writing down
what you knew, you got a few ideas. He scanned Canto
One. "Soft bosoms," he saw. Then "Belinda still her
downy pillow prest." He felt himself quicken. Pope knew
what he was doing, all right. The associations: bosom
and pillow, prest and breast. Niles shut his eyes. He was
weighing Belinda's perfect breasts in his hands, mas-
saging her awake as she lay in her tousled noonday bed.
He imagined her hair spread over her face, full lips,
heavy sleep-bruised eyes. He imagined a slim forearm
raised to ward off Sol's tim'rous ray, Belinda turning
on to her back, stretching. Jesus. Would she have hairy
armpits? he wondered, swallowing. Did they shave their
armpits in the eighteenth century? Would it be like that
Frenchwoman he'd seen on a campsite near Limoges last
summer? In the camp supermarket, wearing only a bikini, reaching up for a tin on a high shelf and exposing

a great hank of armpit hair. Niles groaned. He leant forward and rested his head on his open book. "Belinda," he whispered, "Belinda."

"Everything okay, Quentin?"

He sat up abruptly, banging his knees sharply on the bottom of his desk. It was Bowler, his housemaster, his round, bespectacled face peering at him concernedly, his body canted into the study, pipe clenched between his brown teeth. Why couldn't the bastard knock? Niles swore.

"Trying to write an essay, sir," he said.

"Not that difficult, is it?" Bowler laughed. "Got the team for the league?"

Niles handed it over. Bowler studied it, puffing on his pipe, frowning. Niles looked at the sour blue smoke gathering on the ceiling. Typical bloody Bowler.

"This the best we can do? Are you sure about Grover at scrum-half? Crucial position, I would have thought."

"I think he needs to be pressured a bit, sir."

"Right-ho. You're the boss. See you're down for *Pinafore.*"

"Sorry, sir?"

"*Pinafore. HMS.* The opera. Didn't know you sang, Quentin? Shouldn't have thought it was your line really."

"Thought I'd give it a go, sir."

Bowler left and Niles thought about the opera. Holland had said it was a sure thing with the girls: they only came because they wanted to get off with boys. Niles wondered what they'd be like. Scottish girls from the local grammar school. He'd seen them in town often. Dark-blue uniforms, felt hats, long hair, miniskirts. They all looked older than he—more mature. He experienced a sudden moment of panic. What in God's name would he do? Holland and Panton would be there, everyone would see him. He felt his heart beat with unreasonable speed. It was a kind of proof. There was no change of lying or evading the issue. It would be all too public.

They gathered in the music room behind the new chapel for the first mixed rehearsal. There had been three weeks of tedious afternoon practices during which some semblance of singing ability had been forcibly extracted from them by the efforts of Prothero, the music master. Now, Prothero watched the boys enter with a tired and cynical smile. This was his seventh Gilbert and Sullivan since coming to the school, his third *HMS Pinafore*. Two sets of forms faced each other at one end of the long room. The boys sat down on one set, staring at the empty seats opposite as if they were already occupied.

"Now, gentlemen," Prothero began. "The ladies will be here soon. I don't propose to lecture you any more on the subject. I count on your innate good manners and sense of decorum."

Niles, Holland and Panton sat together. Whispered conversations were going on all around. Niles felt his lungs press against his rib cage. The tension was acute; he felt faint with unfamiliar stress. What if not one of them spoke to him? This was dreadful, he thought, and the girls weren't even here. He looked at the fellow members of the chorus. There were some authentic tenors and basses from the school choir but the rest of them were self-appointed lads, frustrates and sexual braggarts. He could sense their crude desire thrumming through the group as if the forms they were sitting on were charged with a low electric current. He looked at the bright-eyed, snouty, expectant faces, heard whispered obscenities and saw the international language of sexual gesticulation being covertly practised as

if they were a gathering of randy deaf-mutes. He felt
vaguely soiled to be counted among them. Beside him
Holland leaned forward and tapped the shoulder of a
boy in front.

"Bloody Mobo," he said quietly and venomously.
"Didn't you get the message? No queers allowed. What
are you bloody doing here? It's girls we're singing with.
Not lushmen, Mobo. No little lushmen."

"Frig off, Holland," the boy said tonelessly. "I'm in
the choir, aren't I?"

"Bloody choir," Holland repeated, his face ugly with
illogical aggression. "Bloody frigging choir."

Then the girls came in.

No one had heard the bus from town arriving, and
the room, to Niles' startled eyes, seemed suddenly to be
filled with chattering uniformed females. He heard
laughter and giggles, caught flashing glimpses of cheeks
and red mouths, hair and knees, as the other half of
the chorus sat itself down opposite. The boys fired nervous exploratory glances across the two yards of floor
between them. Niles studied his score with commend-
able intensity. He noticed Holland brazenly scrutinis-
ing the girls. Cautiously, Niles raised his eyes and looked
over. They seemed very ordinary, was his first reflection. Dark-blue blazers, short skirts, some black tights.
There was one tall girl with a severe, rather thin face.
Her hair was tied up in an elaborate twisted bun and
at first he thought she was a mistress, but then he saw
her uniform. He scanned the features of the others but
their faces refused to register any individuality; he might
have been staring at a Chinese football team.

Holland bowed his head.

"Mm-mm. I've seen mine," he said in a low voice.
"The blonde in front." He gave a whimper of suppressed desire. Some boys looked round and smiled,

complicity springing up instantly, like recognition. "Right, everybody," Prothero shouted, banging out a chord on the piano. "Page twenty-three, please."

"And I'm never ever sick at sea," Prothero sang.
"What, never?" boomed the chorus of sailors.
"No, never," replied Prothero.
"What, *never*?" the chorus sceptically inquired again.
"Hardly ever," Prothero admitted.
"He's hardly ever sick at sea. . . ."
"Fine," Prothero called. "Good. That'll do for today. Thank you, ladies. Your bus should be outside. Scores on the end of the piano as you go out, please."

The bus was late and the girls had to wait for five minutes outside the chapel. Niles took his time finding his coat in the vestibule and when he went outside, Holland and Panton were already talking to four girls. "Niles, Niles," they shouted as he emerged into the watery sunlight of a February afternoon. "Over here." He walked over, the blood pounding in his ears like surf. Holland stood behind a slim blond girl with moles on her face, Panton by a cheery-looking redhead. Niles approached. One of the two remaining girls was the tall, sharp-faced one he'd seen earlier. The other was small, with wispy fair hair and spectacles.

"This is Quentin," Holland said. "Hero of the rugby field, captain of the squash team. Master flogger extraordinaire."

"Shut up!" Niles exclaimed, appalled at this slander. "You bastard."

"What's a flogger?" Holland's girl asked. Panton was doubled up with mirth. The tall girl looked on expressionlessly.

"Never mind," Holland said. "Sorry, Quent. Little joke. Now, this is Joyce." He indicated Panton's girl. "This is

Helen"—pointing to his own. "And"—he looked at the
tall girl—"Alison? Yes, Alison. And, um . . ."

"Frances," said the small girl.

Niles had moved round to stand beside Alison.
Frances was clearly on her own. She stood undecidedly
for a moment before wandering off without a further
word.

Holland and Panton had instinctively sensed out the
kind of girl they were after. Innuendoes were already
being exchanged with a wanton suggestiveness. Niles
looked at Alison. She was tall. In her high heels slightly
taller than he. She appeared older, in her twenties almost, but the severity of her face was partly an illusion
caused by her schoolmarmy bun. Her skirt was not as
short as Helen's or Joyce's; it stopped two inches above
her knees. Her legs were long and shapely. On the la-
pel of her blazer were numerous badges: three Robert-
son's gollies, a small Canadian maple leaf, a yellow
square, and a blue rectangular one with "monitor"
written on it in plain silver letters. She wore a white shirt
and a tie with the smallest knot in it Niles had ever seen.

He had to say something. He cleared his throat.
"Campaign medals?" he said, pointing to the badges. He
realised his finger was two inches from her right breast
and he snatched his hand away. He thought she gave
the thinnest of smiles in response but he couldn't be
sure.

"Cold, though," he said, huffing and puffing into his
cupped hands.

She rummaged in her blazer pockets. "Cigarette?" she
asked, taking out a packet and offering it to him.

Niles was taken aback by this unselfconsciously adult
gesture. "Christ, no," he said hurriedly. "I mean, we're
not allowed."

But she was already offering them to Joyce and Helen. Alison took out a box of matches and lit the others' cigarettes. For some reason Niles was impressed by the capable way she did this—she obviously smoked a lot. Meanwhile, Holland and Panton aped nicotine starvation. When Joyce and Helen exhaled they chased the clouds of smoke about, beating it into their gaping mouths with their hands as if it were vital oxygen. The girls laughed delightedly.

"What I'd give for a fag," said Holland through gritted teeth.

"Oh yeah?" said lissom Helen.

"Now see what you've done," Niles said to Alison with more accusation in his voice than he'd meant.

Alison laughed briefly.

Niles brushed his teeth, alone at the row of basins. He rinsed his mouth out and went to stand in front of the large mirror by the urinals. He looked at his square face. He rubbed his jaw. He'd need to shave tomorrow. He had to shave every two days now. Somebody shouted "virile!" through the washroom door. Niles whirled round but he didn't see who it was. When he turned back to the mirror his face was red.

He thought about Alison. Everything about her was maddeningly indistinct and ambiguous. All he'd heard her say was "cigarette?" and "bye." It wasn't much to build a relationship on. He had an image of the back of her long legs in their tan tights as she'd climbed onto the bus. He wondered what her breasts were like. Her "soft bosoms."

He sighed and belted his dressing-gown tighter around him. He walked through the quiet, empty house towards his dormitory. A junior came padding down the corridor in pyjamas.

"Where are you going, Payne?" Niles said tiredly.

"For a slash, Niles."

"Where's your bloody slippers and dressing-gown then?"

"Oh, Niles," Payne moaned.

"Get back and bloody put them on."

"Oh, God, Niles, *please*. I just want a pee. I'll only be a second."

"Go on, you little shit." Niles raised his hand menacingly. Payne turned and ran back up the corridor.

Niles walked on towards his dormitory. It was a small one, only eight beds. He opened the door quietly. It was well past lights out. The long room was quite dark. He closed the door softly behind him.

"Okay, folks," came a voice. "Stop flogging. Here's Niles."

"Shut up, Fillery," Niles said. Fillery was fat and wicked. His mother was an actress who lived in Cannes.

"What's she like then, Niles?" Fillery said.

"Who?"

"Who? The bloody bird of course, that's who. *Pinafore*. What's your one like."

"Yeah, go on, Niles," said another voice. "Tell us, what's she like?"

"Shut up. I'm warning you lot."

"Come on, Niles," Fillery said wheedlingly. "I bet she's all right. I bet you got a good one."

Niles got into bed. He lay down and put his hands behind his neck. "She's okay," he said grudgingly. "I'm not complaining." There were soft groans of envy at this. "Not bad, I suppose," he went on. "She's got nice long legs."

"What's her name?"

"Alison."

"Oh, Alison, Alison." People tried out the name on their tongues as if it were a foreign word.

"Tits?" Fillery asked.

"You filthy bugger," Niles said. "Trust bloody Fillery." But Niles felt the lie rise unprompted in his throat. "They're nice, if you must know," he said. "Average size. Sort of pointy, if you know what I mean." There was a chorus of groans at this, deep and despairing. Someone jiggled furiously up and down on his bed, causing the springs to creak and complain.

"Shut up," Niles hissed angrily. "That's your lot. Now get to sleep."

He saw Alison at the next rehearsal a week later. Already people had paired off, Helen and Joyce making straight for Holland and Panton at the first break.

"Fifteen minutes, ladies and gentlemen," Prothero called.

Niles wandered over to Alison. Again he was impressed by her mature looks.

"Hi there," he said, as casually as he could.

"Oh . . . hello." She smiled. "It's, um, Quentin, isn't it?"

Niles hated his name. " 'Fraid so," he said.

"Phew," she said. "Any chance of us having a quiet smoke somewhere?"

They picked their way through the small wood at the back of the chapel. It had rained heavily that morning and the stark trunks of the beech and ash trees were wet and shiny. Alison puffed aggressively at her cigarette. Niles had declined again. He turned up the collar of his blazer and remarked on the inclemency of the season. Alison looked suspiciously at him, as if he were making a joke. Her hair was mid-brown and her skin was very white. She had a thin mouth but her lips were well formed; there was a deep and pronounced dip to her cupid's bow. Niles found this detail endearing, as if somehow this validated his choice of her. His heart seemed to swell with emotion. Their elbows touched as the path narrowed. Niles checked his watch.

"Better not go too far," he said, then paused before adding: "They might get suspicious. . . ."

"Sure," Alison said, flicking her cigarette away. "Smoking like a chimney. I've got Highers in a few months."

"Mmmm," Niles sympathised. "I've got my A's," he said. "Then Oxbridge."

"Are you going to Oxford?" Alison asked. She had a mild Scottish accent; she pronounced the *r* in Oxford.

"Yes," he said. "Well, that's the general idea." He wondered why he'd lied.

"I'm going to Aberdeen," she said.

"Ah."

They walked slowly back to the music room. They were the last to arrive. Holland and Panton looked up admiringly at him as he regained his seat.

"Quent," Holland whispered. "You bloody sex maniac."

"Shagger," Panton accused. "Bloody old shagger, Quent."

"Quiet, please," Prothero called. "If you're quite ready, Niles. Now can we have the ensemble? Jolly tars, female relatives and Josephine: 'Oh joy, oh rapture unforeseen, for now the sky is all serene,' right? Two, three."

"What happened next?" Fillery prompted.

Niles lay in bed. He could sense the entire dormitory waiting in quiet expectancy. Hands on their cocks, he thought.

"We went round the back of the chapel," he continued. "Walked into the wood a bit. We sat down on a

log. Chatted a bit . . . I could feel the atmosphere between us just building up. We were talking about work,
but not talking about it, if you know what I mean. It
was more just something to say."
    "Who made the first move?" Fillery asked.
    "I did, of course. I was talking. Then I stopped, and
looked up. She was looking at me . . . in that sort of
way."
    "Oh, God."
    "She was looking at me, as if to say . . . and we just
sort of moved close together and kissed."
    There was a pause.
    "Get your tongue down?"
    "*Jesus,* Fillery. One-track bloody mind. . . Yeah, yeah,
if you must know every detail. Not at first—the third or
fourth kiss. But it got pretty passionate. Frenching just
about all the time."
    "Stop it! Stop it!" somebody called. "I can't stand it
any more."
    "What else happened?" Fillery implored. "Did you . . .
you know?"
    "We kissed mainly. Hell, we didn't have much time.
She was just sort of running her hand through my hair.
I got a bit of a feel but not much. I'll have to wait until
next week."
    Fillery was quiet. "God, you bastard, Niles," he said.
"You lucky bastard."

On Saturday, after lunch, Holland and Panton bicycled
the three miles to the coast. Helen's family kept a caravan on the caravan site by the beach. Helen and Joyce
had arranged to meet the boys there. Niles was playing
in a first XV rugby match. He heard all about their ex-
ploits later in the afternoon. He was in his study changing out of his rugby kit—the school had lost and he

thought he'd pulled a muscle in his thigh—when Holland and Panton burst in.

"Oh, my God, Quent," Holland crowed. "I don't believe it. It was incredible. They had booze too. I'm pissed." He held up his middle finger. "Sticky finger, Quent. First time."

Niles plucked at his laces. An irrational hatred and resentment for Holland and Panton festered inside him. Holland he didn't mind. Pete was screwing all the time by all accounts. But Panton? He was short-arsed and had spots. Why should he have any luck?

"Get your rocks off then?" he asked without looking up.

"Not this time. They wouldn't let us. But, my God, Nilo, we could, you know, we could. We've got to fix something up."

Niles felt a vast relief. Just feel-ups then. Big bloody deal.

"Here," Holland said. "Almost forgot. A message from Alison. Wey-hey!" With a flourish he handed over a lilac envelope. Niles felt his throat contract. He opened it carefully.

"Any clippings?" Holland asked with a snigger.

"Hardly," Niles said. Holland had a French girl-friend who used to send him cuttings of her pubic hair. They were cherished and passed round like sacred relics. This fact had single-handedly boosted Holland's reputation to near-legendary heights.

" 'Dear Quentin,' " Niles read. " 'I was wondering if by any chance you would like to come and have tea tomorrow (Sunday). I realise this is short notice but if I don't hear from you I'll expect you at four. I hope you can make it. Sincerely, Alison.' "

Niles felt his pulled muscle twitch spasmodically in his thigh. "I hope you can make it." That was good. But "sincerely"? Really!

"What is it, for Christ's sake?" Panton asked.

"Tea," Niles said. "Tomorrow afternoon."

Holland shook his head admiringly. "You got it made, Quent boy. You are home and dry. . . . We must get something fixed up, though. For all of us. After the last performance maybe. Jesus, the bloody show's over in a couple of weeks."

Alison's house was a grey sandstone bungalow at the better end of the small Scottish county town near the school. Niles cycled the six miles there through a fine rainy mist and arrived damp and chilled. He met Alison's parents—Mr. and Mrs. McCullen—and her fourteen-year-old sister, Diane. They sat in a warm, immaculate sitting room and ate scones and pancakes. The family were kind and genial and Niles relaxed almost immediately and made them laugh with anecdotes of school life. He was a great success with Diane. Alison sat quietly for most of the time, occasionally passing round plates or pouring out more tea. She was wearing jeans and a tight pale-blue sweater that gave her a firm breasty look. It was the first time he'd seen her out of uniform and the first time he'd seen her with her hair down. It was long and wavy, dull and thick. It made her look less severe. He felt buoyant with lust and desire, as if he were over-inflated, as if his lungs were crammed with extra capacity of air. He had a sherry before remounting his bike for the long ride back. He reached the school in time for supper.

"I undressed her very slowly," he told the dormitory. "As if she was, sort of fragile, or very weak. I unfastened her bra and I kissed her breasts gently. Then . . . then I pulled down her pants and I told her to stand there while I looked at her. She was very slim. Her breasts were firm with almost perfectly round nipples. . . ."

He swallowed, gazing up unblinkingly at the ceiling as he elaborated his fiction. Even Fillery was silent. "Then I undressed and we got into bed. I ran my hands all over her body. I wanted to make love but, well, we couldn't because I . . . I didn't have a johnny." "I've got dozens," Fillery said. "If you'd only asked me."

"How was I meant to know it would happen?" Niles protested. "That her parents weren't going to be in? I thought it was just an invitation for tea, for God's sake."

Niles, Holland and Panton stood at the back of the assembly hall. They were wearing cadet-force naval bell-bottoms rolled up to mid-calf, singlets and red-spotted neckerchiefs. In front of the stage Prothero was trying to get the school orchestra in tune. On stage Mr. Mulcaster, the art teacher, was applying final touches to his backdrop depicting the poop deck of HMS *Pinafore*. Mulcaster's initials were T. A. M.: Thomas Anthony Mulcaster. He was known as Tampax Tony.

"Christ almighty, look at Tampax," Panton said scornfully. "It's pathetic. I think he's actually painting in a seagull."

"Ah, now that's an original touch," Holland confessed. "Almost as good as his rigging and halyards."

"A seagull," Niles said. "What's it supposed to be doing? Hovering in one spot for the entire course of the play?"

"Oh, no. He's painting in a ship on the horizon. A three-master, me hearties, ar."

"We've got to work something out," Holland said seriously. "We must have something arranged for after the cast party. Think of something, for Christ's sake."

"I've already told you," Panton said. "It's got to be the squash courts. They're ideal."

"Not a chance, mate," Niles said. "Do you know

what would happen to me if we got caught?"

"Yes. You'd lose your squash colours," Panton said with heavy sarcasm.

"Jesus, Nilo," Holland pleaded. "You're captain of squash. You've got the keys. We can lock the doors behind us. No one'll know."

"It's all very well for you. I'll get the bloody boot."

"Come on, Quentin. Think of the orgy we can have. I've got blankets, booze. Look, I promised the girls we'd have a party. They're expecting one. We haven't got much time. It'll all be over after Saturday night. Gone. Finished."

Niles was pondering Holland's use of the word *orgy*.

"Okay," he said. "I'll think about it. But I'm not promising anything, mind."

Alison wore a long, flouncy dress that looked as if it were made out of mattress ticking, and a bonnet. Niles stood beside her in the wings. He could hear the audience taking their seats.

"Like the costume," he said. "Nervous?"

Alison cocked her head. "No, I don't think I am, actually." Niles looked more closely at her. She grew daily more inscrutable. They had seen more of each other during the final run up to the play but he felt that the bizarre intimacy of their first encounter had never been approached. The prospect of inviting her to the party seemed an awesome task.

"Listen," he began. "Some of us are having a little 'do' after the cast party on Saturday night. Wondered if you'd fancy coming. You know, select little gathering."

"Saturday night? After the cast party? Yes, okay."

"And I want you lot to think about me this time tomorrow night," Niles told his cowed and quiescent dormitory, "because"—he paused, exultation setting up a

tremor in his voice—"because this time tomorrow night
I shall be making love. Got that? Making love to a real
girl."

Niles gazed transfixed across the stage at Alison. The
final performance of *HMS Pinafore* was almost over. Mr
Booth, the physics master, as Captain Corcoran sang to
Buttercup—a pre-pubescent boy called Martin—that
wherever she might go, he would never be untrue
to her.
"What, never?" Niles and Alison and the company
wanted to know.
"No, never," asserted Captain Corcoran.
"What . . . *never?*" the cast repeated.
"Well . . ." ad-libbed the Captain. "Hardly ever."
"Hardly ever be untrue to thee-ee-ee . . ." the cast
echoed at full volume.

"I mean, be honest," Holland said to assorted members
of the cast. "It's pretty bloody, really. I mean, how these
people turn up year in year out and pay good money
to see that crap I'll never know." He ate some more of
his cream bun and put his arm around Helen. "Ah,
Quentin, old son," he said as Niles came into the dressing room with a paper cup of Coke for Alison. "A word
in your ear." Niles came over. "I think we can make our
move now. Discreetly, though. See you outside the
squash courts in five minutes."

"Be careful," Niles said to Alison. He held her arm
supportively. "Watch out for these paving stones." Alison's high heels seemed to ring out with unpropitious
clarity as they walked across the courtyard to the squash
courts. It was cold and dark and their breath hung in
the air long enough for them to walk through the thin
clouds before they dispersed. Alison's hair was down and

Niles thought she had never looked so beautiful. Her proximity to him and the thought of what was waiting suddenly seemed to make the simple act of walking hideously complicated. He felt as if a sob were lodged in the back of his throat, ready to spring from his mouth at any moment.

"I'm okay," Alison said, and he released her arm.

Holland and Panton were already there with Helen and Joyce.

"At last," Holland said. "What've you two been up to? Couldn't wait, eh?" Everyone giggled. Niles bent his head more than he needed to unlock the door into the squash courts.

Inside number three court they spread rugs on the boards and sat in a circle round a solitary candle placed in a jam jar. Holland unpacked the picnic. There was some Gouda and Ryvita, a piece of Stilton, slices of salami, gherkins and two long, knobbled Polish sausages. From his coat pockets Panton produced a bottle of South African sherry and half a bottle of gin. Paper cups were distributed and the drinks passed round.

Niles drank some neat gin. "To Gilbert and Sullivan." He toasted the company.

"Ssh," Holland said. "Keep it down, Quentin. Your voice, I mean." There were sniggers at this. Niles didn't dare look at Alison's shadowy face.

They ate their meal with a certain urgent decorum, conscious of the fact that it had to be got out of the way—but in no unseemly rush—before the night's real business could commence. Eventually, after a pre-arranged nod from Holland, Panton said, "Quiet. I think I can hear someone outside." Then he leant forward and blew out the candle. This act was followed by a muffled squeal from Joyce and a flurry of whispered instructions, scuffles and collisions as Holland and Panton, Joyce and Helen, gathered up rugs and paper cups

and groped their way out of the door to their respec-
tive squash courts, leaving number three to Alison and
Niles.

Niles sat in a darkness so total it seemed solid and
shifting, like deep water. He realised he was holding his
breath and let it out slowly. He peered intensely in front
of him, a screen of blasting mental supernova and arc-
ing tracer bullets exploding before his eyes, brighten-
ing the absence of vision. Only the unyielding firmness
of the court floor beneath his buttocks anchored him to
the dimensional world.

He heard Alison move. How close was she?

"Are you all right?" he whispered. He stretched out
his hand, encountering nothing.

"Yes," she said. "Is there anyone?"

"I don't think so. False alarm. Just Panton panick-
ing." His hand touched her shoulder. "Sorry. Can't see
a thing."

"I'm here."

"Oh." The darkness began to retreat. He sensed rather
than saw Alison. He moved across the rug, closer to her.

"Bloody dark."

"Yes."

He moved his head towards her, gently, almost
blindly, like two docking spacecraft. After some soft
bumps and readjustments, their lips connected ten-
uously, then sealed. Niles felt his heart swell to inflate
his chest as he felt her thin cool lips beneath his. This
was the fifth girl he had kissed properly. It remained
as thrilling and exciting as the first time. He wondered
if he would always feel this way. With little grunts and
discreet pressures he managed to lie Alison down on
the rug. Her long hair caught across his face, strands
filling his mouth which he had to pull free with his fingers. They kissed again. Niles felt enormously humble

and reverential. The accumulated sensations of triumph and release in a kiss were almost enough for him really, but he promptly banished such heretical thoughts from his mind. He managed to get both his arms round Alison and he felt her hands move on his back. His head was resting comfortably on his own left shoulder, Alison's head nestled in the crook of his left elbow. Their knees were touching; her face was perhaps three inches away from his. Some faint source of light picked out a curve on a cheekbone, a glimmer in an eye. The warm breath of her exhalations grazed his cheek. What should he do now? he wondered. Had he much time? What would she like him to do? What was she expecting? Perhaps she wanted to make love too? The novelty of this last idea came to him as rather a shock. He felt suddenly vulnerable and insecure; he sensed the alien presence of her femininity descend on and enfold him. He became immediately aware of his vast ignorance about Alison—the person, the girl—separating him ineluctably from her. Despite the fact that they were lying in each other's arms, they might have been facing each other across some great river estuary. The figure on the far bank was a girl's, yes, but that was all he knew.

He felt a gentle shaking. He woke up with a start. His eyes were open but he saw nothing. He sat up. His left arm was dead. It flopped lifelessly at his side.

"You've been asleep," Alison said. "I've got to go."

"What?"

"It's just gone eleven. I've got to get the last bus."

"Jesus. Asleep? You mean I . . . ? How long was . . . ?"

"You just drifted off. You've been sleeping about half an hour. I didn't want to wake you."

Niles felt shame and disgrace cause tears to prickle

at the corner of his eyes. He picked up his left hand and started to massage it. In the darkness it was like holding an amputated limb. To his right hand his nerveless left felt rough and calloused, like a stranger's.

"Can you find the door?"

They went outside. Alison wondered about the remains of the picnic. Niles told her he'd clean up in the morning before anyone came.

He was about to lock the door. "What about the others?" he asked, fighting to keep the bitterness from his voice.

"They left about ten minutes ago. I heard them going."

Niles locked the squash court door. He gazed bleakly round him. Alison stood patiently, knotting her scarf at her throat. It was a sharp, frosty night. The school buildings loomed on either side, dark and unpeopled.

"I'd better go, Quentin," Alison said.

"I'll come with you to the bus stop."

They sat out together, Niles looking nervously back over his shoulder. He was taking a calculated risk. The bus stop lay half a mile beyond the school gates. If he was caught out of bounds with a girl at this time of night he would be in serious trouble. But equally he felt that whatever happened, nothing should prevent him from being with Alison at this moment. They walked on in silence. Niles' mind was a tangle of conflicting emotions. Sentences formed in his head, only to split into whirling separate words like some modish animated film. He felt he should say something, explain that he hadn't meant to fall asleep, allude to his romantic plans, but his tongue and his mind refused to co-ordinate. His brain seemed to lock into an imbecilic stupidity. He couldn't do anything right.

At the school gates he let Alison stride confidently

through and go a little way down the road before he
snaked beneath the lodge windows, squirmed through
the side gate and made a sequence of zigzag dashes from
bush to tree trunk, like a commando behind enemy lines,
before he caught up with her.

Alison stood in the middle of the road waiting for him.
"That's a bit dramatic, isn't it?"

"I'm out of bounds, you see. If I get caught . . ."

"I don't want you to get into trouble, Quentin."

"Forget it, really. I don't care." He took her hand.
There was a small shelter by the bus stop. . . . "Come
on, let's go." They walked briskly down the road.

The shelter was empty. A nearby street light threw
the graffiti carved on its green wooden bench into high
relief. Small drifts of cigarette packs, soft-drink cans and
wrappers were banked beneath it.

"Alison," Niles began. "Listen. I have to say this. I
don't want you to think that . . ."

"Here it comes," cried Alison, as the bus appeared
round the corner. "That was lucky."

The bus stopped. She gave him a swift kiss on the
cheek, so swift it was almost a clash of heads, and got
on. Niles looked at the single-decker bus. Inside, it was
soft-yellow and smoky. A couple of old women looked
curiously back at him. On the rear seats some louts drank
beer from cans. Alison stood at the top of the steps, her
back to him, buying her ticket from the driver. Her long
legs seemed twin symbols of rebuke.

"I'll phone," he shouted, louder than he meant. It
sounded like a grievance, a threat. She turned, smiled,
and walked down the bus to take her seat. Niles saw her
thick dark hair on her blazer, saw her head toss as she
sat down. She waved. The bus drove off. He didn't wave
back.

Niles walked morosely up the drive. He walked on

the verge, ready to duck behind one of the beech trees that lined the road should a car come by. He stumbled over a root, stopped, turned and kicked savagely at it. In a sombre mood of reassessment he cursed his school, the closed society he was compelled to live in, his demanding, predatory, so-called friends. "Women," his father had once patronisingly told him, "are a lifetime's study." He was off to a late start then, he observed grimly, and wondered if he would ever catch up. He felt suddenly exhausted by the daily, monotonous absorption with sex, disgusted by the lonely idolatry of masturbation. He felt that his sexual nature, whatever it might be, was irretrievably corrupted.

He paused and took a few deep breaths, trying to shake the mood from him. At this point the drive curved gently to the right, back towards main school. On his left and ahead of him lay a wide flat expanse of playing fields, fixed and still under a faint starlight. His house lay in that direction. It would be quicker, but he wondered if he dared expose himself on the open space. He made up his mind. He set off, breaking into a steady jog, feeling the frost cracking under his feet, puffing his condensed breath ahead of him like a steam engine. He loped silently and strongly across the pitches. He felt that he could run for ever. He would be back in the dorm before twelve. They would all be waiting for him. Fillery had said they'd stay up specially. They wanted to know everything, Fillery had said, every little detail. The bastards, Niles said to himself, smiling. His mind began to work. He'd give them a good story tonight, all right. They wouldn't forget this one in a long time. He ran on, a strange jubilation lengthening his stride.

The Care and Attention
of Swimming Pools

Listen to this. Read it to yourself. Out loud. Read it slow and think about it.

> A swimming pool is like a child,
> Leave it alone and it will surely run wild.

Who said that? Answer: Me. I did.

WINTERING

"Can I swim?" says Noelle-Joy. "It's a fantastic pool."

Much as I would like to see her jugs in a swimsuit, I have to say no.

"Aw. Pretty please? Why not?"

"I'm afraid the pool is wintering."

Noelle-Joy squints skeptically up at the clear blue sky. There's not even any smog today. She exposes the palms of her hands to the sun's powerful rays.

"But it's *hot,* man. Anyways, we don't get no winter in L.A.," she argues.

Patiently I explain that, four seasons or no, every pool has to winter. A period of rest. What you might call a pool-sabbath. I've lowered the water level below the skimmers, surchlorinated, and washed out my cartridge filter. A pool, as I explain several times a day to my clients, is not just a hole in the ground filled with water. Wintering removes constant wear and tear, rests the incessantly churning pump machinery, allows essential repairs and maintenance, permits cleansing of the canals, filter system and heating units. You can't do all that if you're splashing around in the goddam thing. Most people realize I'm talking sense.

We walk around my pool. It's small but it's got everything. No-Skid surrounds, terrace lights, skimmers, springboard, all-weather poolside furniture, and a bamboo cocktail bar plus hibachi. I've got to admit it looks kind of peculiar stuck in my little backyard. (In this part of the city it's the only private pool for seventeen blocks.) But so what! I busted my balls for that little baby. I got me a new vacuum sweep last month. I'm aiming for a sand filter now, to replace my old cartridge model.

I stand proudly behind the bar and pour Noelle-Joy a drink. She's wearing a yellow halter-neck and tight purple shorts. Maybe if she were a little thinner they'd look a bit better on her . . . I don't know. If you got it, flaunt it, I guess. Her legs are kind of short and her thighs have got that strange rumpled look. She stacks her red hair high on top of her head to compensate. She lights a Kool, sips her drink, sighs and hugs herself. Then she sees my hibachi and screams. I drop my cocktail shaker.

"My God! A hibachi. Permanent as well. Hey, can we barbecue? Please? Don't tell me that's wintering too."

I ignore her sarcasm. "Sure," I say, picking up ice cubes. "Come by tomorrow."

***

I work for AA1 Pools (Maintenance) Inc. We've also been
ABC Pools and Aardvark Pools. I tell my boss, Sol Yorty,
that we should call ourselves something like Azure
Dreams, Paradise Pools, Still Waters—that kind of name.
Yorty laughs and says it's better to be at the head of the
line in the Yellow Pages than sitting on our butts, poor,
with some wise-ass, no-account trademark. The man has
no pride in his work. If I wasn't up to my ears in hock
to him I'd quit and set up on my own. TROPICAL LA-
GOONS, BLUE DIAMOND POOLS . . . I haven't settled on
a name yet. The name is important.

GREEN WATER

Down Glendale Boulevard, Hollywood Freeway, onto
Santa Monica Freeway. Got the ocean coming up. Left
into Brentwood. Client lives off Mandeville Canyon. My
God, the houses in Brentwood. The *pools* in Brentwood. You've never seen swimming pools like them. All
sizes, all shapes, all eras. But nobody looks after them.
I tell you, if pools were animate, Brentwood would be
a national scandal.

The old Dodge van stalls on the turn up into the
driveway. Yorty's got to get a new van soon, for Christ's
sake. I leave it there.

The house stands at the top of a green ramp of lawn
behind a thick laurel hedge. It's a big house, Spanish
colonial revival style with half-timbered English Tudor
extension. A Hispanic manservant takes me down to the
pool. "You wait here," he says. Greaser. I don't like his
tone. One thing I've noticed about this job, people think
a pool cleaner is lower than a snake's belly. They look
right through you. I was cleaning a pool up on Palos
Verdes once. This couple started balling right in front
of me. No kidding.

The pool. Thirty yards by fifteen. Grecian pillared pool house and changing rooms. Marble-topped bar. Planted around with oleanders. I feel the usual sob build up in my throat. It's quiet. There's a small breeze blowing. I dip my hand in the water and shake it around some. The sun starts dancing on the ripples, wobbling lozenges of light, wavy chicken-wire shadows on the blue tiles. What is it about swimming pools? Just sit beside one, with a cold beer in your hand, and you feel happy. It's like some kind of mesmeric influence. A trance. I said to Yorty once: "Give everybody their own pool to sit beside and there'd be no more trouble in this world." The fat moron practically bust a gut.

I myself think it's something to do with the color of the water. That blue. I always say that they should call that blue "swimming pool blue." Try it on your friends. Say "swimming pool blue" to them. They know what you mean right off. It's a special color. The color of tranquillity. Got it! TRANQUILLITY POOLS . . . Yeah, that's it.. Fuck Yorty.

But the only trouble with this particular pool is it's *green*. The man's got green water.

"Hey!" I hear a voice. "You come for the pool?"

I'm only wearing coveralls with AA1 POOLS written across the back in red letters. This guy's real sharp. He comes down the steps from the house, his joint just about covered with a minute black satin triangle. He's swinging a bullworker in one hand. Yeah, he's big. Shoulders like medicine balls, bulging overhang of pectorals. His chest is shiny and completely hairless, with tiny brown nipples almost a yard apart. But his eyes are set close together. I guess he's been using the bullworker on his brain too. I've seen him on the TV. Biff Ruggiero, ex-pro football star.

"Mr Ruggiero?"

"Yeah, that's me. What's wrong wit da pool?"

"You got green water. Your filtration's gone for sure. You got a buildup of algae. When was the last time you had things checked out?"

He ignored my question. "Green water? Shit, I got friends coming to stay tomorrow. Can you fix it?"

"Can you brush your teeth? Sure I can fix it. But you'd better not plan on swimming for a week."

". . . and this stupid asshole, Biff Ruggiero—you know, pro footballer?—he hangs around all day asking dumb questions. 'Whatcha need all dat acid for?' So there I am, I'm washing out his friggin' cartridges with phosphate tri-soda, and all this crap's like coming out. 'Holy Jesus,' says Mr. Nobel Prize-winner, 'where's all dat shit come from?' Jesus." I laugh quietly to myself. "He's so dumb he thinks Fucking is a city in China."

I watch Noelle-Joy get out of bed. She stands for a while rubbing her temples.

"I'm going to take a shower," she says.

I follow her through to the bathroom.

"It just shows you," I shout over the noise of the water. "Those cartridge filters may be cheap but they can be a real pain in the nuts. I told him to put in a sand filter like the one I'm getting. Six-way valve, automatic rinsage—"

Noelle-Joy bursts out of the closet, her little stacked body all pink from the shower. She heads back into the bedroom, towels off and starts to dress.

"Hey, baby," I say. "Listen. I thought of a great name. Tranquillity Pools." I block out the letters in the air. "Trang. Quill. It. Tee. Tranquillity Pools. What do you think?"

"Look," she says, her gaze flinging around the room. "Ah. I gotta, um, do some shopping. I'll catch up with you later, okay?"

Noelle-Joy moves in. Boy, dames sure own a lot of garbage. She works as a stapler in a luggage factory. We get on fine. But already she's bugging me to get a car. She doesn't like to be seen in the Dodge van. She's a sweet girl, but there are only two things Noelle-Joy thinks about. Money, and more money. She says I should ask Yorty for a raise. I say how am I going to do that seeing I'm already in to him for a $5,000 sand filter. She says she wouldn't give the steam off her shit for a sand filter. She's a strong-minded woman but her heart's in the right place. She loves the pool.

"You look after this pool great, you know," Ruggiero says. I'm de-ringing the sides with an acid wash. We cleaned up the green water weeks ago but we've got a regular maintenance contract with him now.

"I never realized, like, they was so complicated."

I shoot him my rhyme.

"That's good," Ruggiero says, scratching his chin. "Say, you wanna work for me, full time?"

I tell him about my plans. Tranquillity Pools, the new sand filter, Noelle-Joy.

I come home early. An old lady called up from out in Pacific Palisades. She said her dog had fallen into her pool in the night. She said she was too upset to touch it. I had to fish it out with the long-handled pool sieve. It was one of those tiny hairy dogs. It had sunk to the bottom. I dragged it out and threw it in the garbage can.

"No poolside light, lady," I said. "You don't light the way, no wonder your dog fell in. If that'd got sucked into the skimmers you'd have scarfed up your entire filter system. Bust valves, who knows?"

Wow, did she take a giant shit on me. Called Yorty,

the works. I had to get the mutt's body out of the trash can, wash it, lay it out on a cushion. . . . No wonder I'm red-assed when I get home.

Noelle-Joy's out by the pool working on her tan. Fruit punch, shades, orange bikini, pushed-up breasts. There's a big puddle of water underneath the sun-lounger.

"Hi, honey," she calls, stretching. "This is the life, yeah?"

I go mad. "You been in the water?" I yell.

"What? . . . Yeah. So I had a little swim. So big deal."

"How many times I got to tell you. The pool's wintering."

"The pool's been wintering for *three fuckin' months!*" she screams.

But I'm not listening. I run into the pool house. Switch on the filters to full power. I grab three pellets of chlorine—no, four—and throw them in. Then I get the sack of soda ash, tip in a couple of spadefuls just to be sure.

I stand at the pool edge panting.

"What do you think you're doing?" she accuses.

"Superchlorination," I say. "You swam in stagnant water. Who knows what you could've brought in."

Now she goes mad. She stomps up to me. "I just *swam* in your fuckin' pool, turd-bird! I didn't piss in it or nothing!"

I've got her there. "I know you didn't," I yell in triumph. " 'Cause I can tell. I got me a secret chemical in that water. *Secret.* Anybody pisses in my pool it turns *black!*"

We made up, of course. "A lovers' tiff" is the expression, I believe. I explain why I was so fired up. Noelle-Joy is all quiet and thoughtful for an hour or two. Then she asks me a favor. Can she have a housewarming party

for all her friends? There's no way I can refuse. I say
yes. We are real close that night.

OTO

OTO. I don't know how we ever got by without OTO,
or orthotolodine, to give its full name. We use it in the
Aquality Duo Test. That's how we check the correct
levels of chlorination and acidity (pH) in a pool. If you
don't get it right you'd be safer swimming in a cesspit.
I'm doing an OTO test for Ruggiero. He's standing
there crushing a tennis ball in each hand. His pool is
looking beautiful. He's got some guests around it—lean,
tanned people. Red umbrellas above the tables. Rock
music playing from the speakers. Light from the water
winking at you. That chlorine smell. That fresh cool-
ness you get around pools.

One thing I will say for Ruggiero, he doesn't treat me
like some sidewalk steamer. And the man seems to be
interested in what's going on.

I show him the two little test tubes lined up against
the color scales.

"Like I said, Mr. Ruggiero, it's perfect. OTO never
lets you down. You always know how your pool's
feeling."

"Hell," Ruggiero says, "looks like you got to be a
chemist to run a pool. Am I right or am I right?" He
laughs at his joke.

I smile politely and step back from the pool edge,
watch the water dance.

"A thing of beauty, Mr. Ruggiero, is a joy forever.
Know who said that? An English poet. I don't need to
run no OTO test. I been around pools so long I got an
instinct about them. I know how they feel. Little too
much acid, bit of algae, wrong chlorine levels . . . I see
them, Mr. Ruggiero, and they tell me."

"Come on," Ruggiero says, a big smile on his face. "Let me buy you a drink."

Sol Yorty looks like an aging country-and-western star. He's bald on top but he's let his gray hair grow over his ears. He lives in dead-end East Hollywood. I walk down the path in his back garden with him. Yorty's carrying a bag of charcoal briquettes. His fat gut stretches his lime-green sports shirt skintight. He and his wife, Dolores, are the fattest people I know. Between them they weigh as much as a small car. The funny thing about Yorty is that even though he owns a pool company he doesn't own a pool.

He tips the briquettes into his barbecue as I explain that I'm going to have to hold back on the sand filter for a month or two. This party of Noelle-Joy's is going to make it hard for me to meet the deposit.

"No problem," Yorty says. "Glad to see you're making a home at last. She's a . . . She seems like a fine girl." He lays out four huge steaks on the grill.

"Oh, sorry, Sol," I say. "I didn't know you had company. I wouldn't have disturbed you."

"Nah," he says. "Just me and Dolores." He looks up as Dolores waddles down the garden in a pair of flaming-orange Bermudas and the biggest bikini top I've ever seen.

"Hey, sweetie," he shouts. "Look who's here."

Dolores carries a plastic bucket full of rice salad. "Well, hi, stranger. Wanna eat lunch with us? There's plenty more in the fridge."

I say I've got to get back.

It looks like Noelle-Joy's invited just about the entire work force from the luggage factory. Mainly guys, too, a few blacks and Hispanics. The house is crammed with guests. You can't move in the yard. This morning I

vacuum-swept the pool, topped up the water level, got
the filters going well and threw in an extra pellet of
chlorine. You can't be too sure. Some of Noelle-Joy's
friends don't seem too concerned about personal hy-
giene. Everybody, though, is being real nice to me.
Noelle-Joy and I stand at the door greeting the guests.
Noelle-Joy makes the introductions. Everyone smiles
broadly and we shake hands.

I feel on edge as the first guests dive into the pool. I
watch the water slosh over the sides, darkening the No-
Skid surrounds. I hear the skimmer valves clacking
madly. Noelle-Joy squeezes my hand. She's been very affectionate these last few days. Now every few minutes she
comes on over from talking to her friends and asks me
if I'm feeling fine. She keeps smiling and looking at me.
But it's what I call her lemon smile—like she's only
smiling with her lips. Maybe she's nervous, too, I think,
wondering what her friends from the luggage factory
will make of me.

I have to say I'm not too disappointed though, when
I'm called away by the phone. It's from Mr. Ruggiero's
house. Something's gone wrong; there's some sort of
sediment in the water. I think fast. I say it could be a
precipitation of calcium salts and I'll be there right away.

I clap my hands for silence at the poolside. Everyone
stops talking.

"I'm sorry, folks," I say. "I have to leave you for a
while. I got an emergency on. You all just keep right
on having a good time. I'll be back as soon as I can.
Bye now."

Traffic's heavy at this time of the day. We've got a grid-
lock at Western Avenue and Sunset. I detour around
on the Ventura Freeway, out down through Beverly
Glen, back onto Sunset and on into Brentwood.

I run down the back lawn to the pool. I can see Ruggiero and some of his friends splashing around in the water. Stupid fools. The Hispanic manservant tries to stop me but I just lower my shoulder and bulldoze through him.

"Hey!" I shout. "Get the fuck out of that water! Don't you know it's dangerous? Get out, everybody, get out!"

Ruggiero's muscles launch him out of the pool like a dolphin.

"What's goin' on?" He looks angry and puzzled. "You ain't a million laughs, you know, man."

I'm on my knees peering at the water. The other guests have clambered out and are looking around nervously. They think of plagues and pollution.

In front of my nose the perfect translucent water bobbs and shimmies; nets of light wink and flash in my eyes.

"The sediment," I say. "The calcium salts . . . didn't somebody phone. . . ?"

By the time I get back I've been away for nearly an hour and a half. She worked fast, I have to admit. Cleaned out everything. She and her friends—they had it all planned. I'd been deep-sixed for sure.

There was a note. YOU MAY NO A LOT A BOUT POOLS BUT YOU DONT NO SHIT A BOUT PEPLE.

I don't want to go out to the yard but I know I have to. I walk through the empty house like I'm walking knee-deep in wax. The yard is empty. I can see they threw everything in the pool—the loungers, the tables, the bamboo cocktail bar, bobbing around like the remains from a shipwreck. Then all of them standing in a circle around the side, laughing, having their joke.

I walk slowly up to the edge and look down. I can see my reflection. The water's like black coffee.

***

Yorba Linda. It's just off the Riverside Expressway. I'm working as a cleaner at the public swimming pool. Open air, Olympic-sized.

Yorty had to fire me after what he heard from Ruggiero. Sol said he had no choice. He was sorry but he would "have to let me go."

I sold up and moved out after the party. That pool could never be the same after what they had done in it. I don't know—it had lost its innocence, I guess.

Funny thing happened. I was standing on Sunset and a van halted at an intersection. It was a Ford, I think. It was blue. I didn't get a look at the driver, but on the side, in white letters, was TRANQUILLITY POOLS. The van drove off before I could get to it. I'm going to file a complaint. Somebody's stolen my name.

Killing Lizards

Gavin squatted beside Israel, the cook's teenage son, on the narrow verandah of the servants' quarters. Israel was making Gavin a new catapult. He bound the thick rubber thongs to the wooden Y with string, tying the final knot tight and nipping off the loose ends with his teeth. Gavin took the proffered catapult and tried a practice shot. He fired at a small grove of banana trees by the kitchen garden. The pebble thunked into a fibrous bole with reassuring force.

"Great!" Gavin said admiringly, then "Hey!" as Israel snatched the catapult back. He dangled the weapon alluringly out of Gavin's reach and grinned as the small twelve-year-old boy leapt angrily for it.

"Cig'rette. Give me cig'rette," Israel demanded, laughing in his high, wheezy way.

"Oh, all right," Gavin grudgingly replied, handing over the packet he had stolen from his mother's handbag the day before. Israel promptly lit one and confidently puffed smoke up into the washed-out blue of the African sky.

Gavin walked back up the garden to the house. He was a thin, dark boy with a slightly pinched face and unusually thick eyebrows that made his face seem older than it was. He went through the kitchen and into the cool, spacious living room, with its rugs and tiled floor,

where two roof fans energetically beat the hot afternoon air into motion.

The room was empty and Gavin walked along the
verandah past his bedroom and that of his older sister.
His sister, Amanda, was at boarding school in England;
Gavin was going to join her there next year. He used
to like his sister but since her fifteenth birthday she had
changed. When she had come out on holiday last
Christmas she had hardly played with him at all. She
was bored with him; she preferred going shopping with
her mother. A conspiracy of sorts seemed to have sprung
up between the women of the family from which Gavin
and his father were excluded.

When he thought of his sister now, he felt that he
hated her. Sometimes he wished the plane that was
bringing her out to Africa would crash and she would
be killed. Then there would be only Gavin; he would
be the only child. As he passed her bedroom he was reminded of this fantasy and despite himself he paused,
thinking about it again, trying to imagine what life would
be like—how it would be different. As he did so, the
other dream began to edge itself into his mind like an
insistent hand signalling at the back of a classroom,
drawing attention to itself. He had this dream quite a
lot these days and it made him feel peculiar; he knew
it was bad, a wrong thing to do, and sometimes he forced
himself not to think about it. But it never worked, for
it always came faltering back with its strange imaginative allure, and he would find himself lost in it, sa-
vouring its pleasures, indulging in its sweet, illicit
sensations.

It was a variation on the theme of his sister's death,
but this time it also included his father. His father and
sister had died in a car crash and Gavin had to break
the news to his mother. As she sobbed with grief she

clung to him for support. Gavin would soothe her, stroking her hair as he'd seen done on TV in England, whispering words of comfort.

In the dream Gavin's mother never remarried, and she and Gavin returned to England to live. People would look at them in the street, the tall elegant widow in black, and her son, growing tall and more mature himself, being brave and good by her side. People around them seemed to whisper: "I don't know what she would have done without him," and, "Yes, he's been a marvel," and, "They're so close now."

Gavin shook his head, blushing guiltily. He didn't hate his father—he just got angry with him sometimes—and it made him feel bad and upset that he kept on imagining him dead. But the dream insistently repeated itself, and it continued to expand; the narrative furnished itself with more and more precise details; the funeral scene was added, the cottage Gavin and his mother took near Canterbury, the plans they made for the school holidays. It grew steadily more real and credible—it was like discovering a new world—but as it did, so Gavin found himself more dissatisfied with the way things were.

Gavin slowly pushed open the door of his parents' bedroom. Sometimes he knocked, but his mother had laughed and told him not to be silly. Still, he was cautious, as he had once been horribly embarrassed to find them both asleep, naked and sprawled on the rumpled double bed. But today he knew his father was at work in his chemistry lab. Only his mother would be having a siesta.

But Gavin's mother was sitting in front of her dressing table brushing her short but thick reddish auburn hair. She was wearing only a black bra and pants that contrasted strongly with the pale freckly tan of her firm body. A cigarette burned in an ashtray. She brushed methodically and absent-mindedly, her shining hair crackling under the brush. She seemed quite unaware of Gavin standing behind her, looking on. Then he coughed.

"Yes, darling, what is it?" she said without looking round.

Gavin sensed rather than appreciated that his mother was a beautiful woman. He did not realise that she was prevented from achieving it fully by a sulky turn to her lips and a hardness in her pale eyes. She stood up and stretched languidly, walking barefooted over to the wardrobe, where she selected a cotton dress.

"Where are you going?" Gavin asked without thinking.

"Rehearsal, dear. For the play," his mother replied.

"Oh. Well, I'm going out too." He left it at that. Just to see if she'd say anything this time, but she seemed not to have heard. So he added, "I'm going with Laurence and David. To kill lizards."

"Yes, darling," his mother said, intently examining the dress she had chosen. "Do try not to touch the lizards. They're nasty things. There's a good boy." She held the dress up in front of her and looked at her reflection critically in the mirror. She laid the dress on the bed, sat down again and began to apply some lipstick. Gavin looked at her rich red hair and the curve of her spine in her creamy back, broken by the dark strap of her bra, and the three moles on the curve of her haunch where it was tautened by the elastic of her pants. Gavin swallowed. His mother's presence in his life loomed like a huge wall at whose foot his needs cowered like beggars at a city gate. He wished she bothered about him more, did things with him as she did with Amanda. He felt strange and uneasy about her, proud and uncomfortable. He had been pleased last Saturday when she took him to the pool in town, but then she had worn a small bikini and the Syrian men round the bar had stared at her. (David's mother always wore a swimsuit of a prickly material with stiff bones in it.) When he went out of the room she was brushing her hair again and he didn't bother to say goodbye.

Gavin walked down the road. He was wearing a striped T-shirt, white shorts and Clarks sandals without socks. The early afternoon sun beat down on his head and the heat vibrated up from the tarmac. On either side of him were the low senior-staff bungalows, shadowy beneath their wide eaves. They seemed to be pressed down into the earth, as if the blazing sun bore down with intolerable weight. The coruscating scarlet dazzle of flamboyant trees that lined the road danced spottily in his eyes.

The university campus was a large one but Gavin had come to know it intimately in the two years since his parents had moved to Africa. In Canterbury his father had been only a lecturer but here he was a professor in the Chemistry Department. Gavin loved to go down to the labs with their curious ammoniacal smells, brilliant fluids and mad-scientist constructions of phials, test-tubes and rubber pipes. He thought he might pay his father a surprise visit that afternoon, as their lizard hunt should take them in that direction.

Gavin and his two friends had been shooting lizards with their catapults for the three weeks of the Easter holidays and had so far accounted for 143. They killed mainly the male and female of one species that seemed to populate every group of boulders or area of concrete in the country. The lizards were large, sometimes growing to eighteen inches in length. The females were slightly smaller than the males and were a dirty speckled-khaki colour. The males were more resplendent, with brilliant orange-red heads, pale-grey bodies and black-barred feet and tails. They did no one any harm, just basked in the sun doing a curious bobbing press-up motion. At first they were ludicrously easy to kill. The boys could creep up to within three or four feet and with one well-placed stone reduce the basking, complacent lizard to a writhing knot, its feet clawing at a buckled spine or shattered head. A slight guilt had soon grown up among the boys and they accordingly convinced themselves that the lizards were pests and that, rather like rats, they spread diseases.

But the lizards, like any threatened species, grew wise to the hunters and now scurried off at the merest hint of approach, and the boys had to range wider and wider through the campus to find zones where the word had not spread and where the lizards still clung unconcernedly to walls, like dozing sunbathers unaware of the looming thunderclouds.

Gavin met his friends at the pre-arranged corner. Today they were heading for the university staff's preparatory school at a far edge of the campus. There was an expansive outcrop of boulders there with a sizeable lizard community that they had been evaluating for some time, and this afternoon they planned a blitz.

They walked down the road firing stones at trees and clumps of bushes. Gavin teased Laurence about his bandy legs and then joined forces with him to mock David about his spots and his hugely fat sister until he threatened to go home. Gavin felt tense and malicious, and lied easily to them about how he had fashioned his own catapult, which was far superior to their clumsier home-made efforts. He was glad when they rounded a corner and came in sight of the long simple buildings of the chemistry labs.

"Let's go and see my dad," he suggested.

Gavin's father was marking exam papers in an empty lab when the three boys arrived. He was tall and thin with sparse black hair brushed across his balding head. Gavin possessed his similar tentative smile. They chatted for a while; then Gavin's father showed them some frozen nitrogen. He picked a red hibiscus bloom off a hedge outside and dipped it in the container of fuming liquid. Then he dropped the flower on the floor and it shattered to pieces like fine china.

"Where are you off to?" he asked as the boys made ready to leave.

"Down to the school to get lizards," Gavin replied.

"There's a monster one down there," said David. "I've seen it."

"I hope you don't leave them lying around," Gavin's father said. "Things rot in this sun very quickly."

"It's okay," Gavin affirmed brightly. "The hawks soon get them."

Gavin's father looked thoughtful. "What's your mother doing?" he asked his son. "Left her on her own, have you?"

"Israel's there," Gavin replied sullenly. "But anyway she's going to her play rehearsal or something. Drama, drama, you know."

"Today? Are you sure?" his father asked, seemingly surprised.

"That's what she said. Bye, Dad. See you tonight."

The school lay on a small plateau overlooking a teak forest and the jungle that stretched away beyond it. The outcrop of rocks was poised on the edge of the plateau and it ran down in pale, pinkish slabs to the beginning of the teak trees.

The boys killed four female lizards almost at once but the others had rushed into crevices and stayed there. Gavin caught a glimpse of a large red head as it scuttled off, and the three of them pelted the deep niche it hid in and prodded at it with sticks, but it was just not coming out.

Then Gavin and Laurence thought they saw a fruit bat in a palm tree, but David couldn't see it and soon lost interest. They patrolled the deserted school buildings for a while and then hung, bat-like themselves, on the jungle gym in the playground. David, who had perched on the top, heard the sound of a car as it negotiated a bumpy rutted track that led into the jungle and which ran for a while along the base of the plateau. He soon saw a Volkswagen van lurching along. A man was driving and a woman sat beside him.

"Hey, Gavin," David said without thinking. "Isn't that your mother?"

Gavin climbed quickly up beside him and looked.

"No," he said. "Nope. Definitely."

They resumed their play but the implication hung in the air like a threat, despite their suddenly earnest jocularity. In the unspoken way in which these things arrange themselves, David and Laurence soon announced that they had to go home. Gavin said that he would stay on a bit. He wanted to see if he could get that big lizard.

Laurence and David wandered off with many a backward-shouted message about where they would meet tomorrow and what they would do. Then Gavin clambered about half-heartedly on the jungle gym before he walked down the slope to the track, which he followed into the teak forest. There was still heat in the afternoon sun and the trees and bushes looked tired from a day's exposure. The big soup-plate leaves of the teak trees hung limply in the damp, dusty atmosphere.

Gavin heard his mother's laugh before he saw the van. He moved off the track and followed the curve of a bend until he saw the van through the leaves. It was pulled up on the other side of the mud road. The large sliding door was thrown back and Gavin could see that the bunk bed inside had been folded down. His mother was sitting on the edge of the bunk, laughing. A man without a shirt was struggling to zip up her dress. She laughed again, showing her teeth and throwing back her head, joyously shaking her thick red hair. Gavin knew the man: he was called Ian Swan and sometimes came to the house. He had a neat black beard and curling black hair all over his chest.

Gavin stood motionless behind the thick screen of leaves and watched his mother and the man. He knew at once what they had been doing. He watched them caper and kiss and laugh. Finally Gavin's mother tugged herself free and scrambled round the van and into the front seat. Gavin saw a pair of sunglasses drop from her open handbag. She didn't notice they had fallen. Swan put on his shirt and joined her in the front of the van.

As they backed and turned the van Gavin held his breath in an agony of tension in case they should run over the glasses. When they had gone he stood for a while before walking over and picking up the sunglasses. They were quite cheap; Gavin remembered she had bought them last leave in England. They were favourites. They had pale blue lenses and candy-pink frames. He held them carefully in the palm of his hand as if he were holding an injured bird.

MUMMY . . .

As he walked down the track to the school, the numbness, the blank camera stare that had descended on him the moment he had heard his mother's high laugh, began to dissipate. A slow tingling charge of triumph and elation began to infuse his body.

OH, MUMMY, I THINK . . .

He looked again at the sunglasses in his palm. Things would change now. Nothing would be the same after this secret. It seemed to him now as if he were carrying a ticking bomb.
OH, MUMMY, I THINK I'VE FOUND YOUR SUNGLASSES.

The lowering sun was striking the flat rocks of the outcrop full on and Gavin could feel the heat through the soles of his sandals as he walked up the slope. Then, ahead, facing away from him, he saw the lizard. It was catching the last warmth of the day, red head methodically bobbing, sleek torso and long tail motionless. Carefully Gavin set down the glasses and took his catapult and a pebble from his pocket. Stupid lizard, he thought, sunbathing, head bobbing like that, you never know who's around. He drew a bead on it, cautiously easing the thick rubber back to full stretch until his rigid left arm began to quiver from the tension.

He imagined the stone breaking the lizard's back, a pink welling tear in the pale scaly skin. The curious slow-motion way the mortally wounded creatures keeled over, sometimes a single leg twitching crazily like a spinning rear wheel on an upended crashed car.

The lizard basked on, unaware.

Gavin eased off the tension. Holding his breath with the effort, heart thumping in his ears. He stood for a few seconds letting himself calm down. His mother would be home now; he should have enough time before his father returned. He picked up the sunglasses and backed softly away and around, leaving the lizard undisturbed. Then, with his eyes alight and gleaming beneath his oddly heavy brows, he set off steadily for home.

Bizarre Situations

Before we start, something from this book I'm reading called *Truth, Falsehood and Philosophy:* "It occasionally happens that a situation is so new and unusual that no speaker of the language is equipped to say what words are appropriate for it. We shall call such situations *bizarre.*"

That's what the book says, and I think it's quite interesting and fairly relevant. But, how to begin? Perhaps:

> I shall never forget the sight of Joan's crumpled body, her head clumsily de-topped, like a fractious child's attempt to open a boiled egg; as if some giant's teaspoon had levered and battered its way to Joan's decidedly average brain.

Or maybe:

> I am here in Paris, Monday night, Bar Cercle, Rue Christine—well into my third Pernod—looking for Kramer. Kramer who came to stay and allowed his wife to suicide in my guest bedroom. Suicide? No chance. Kramer murdered her and I have the proof. I think.

Or possibly:

To cure some chronic cases of epilepsy, surgeons sometimes resort to a severance of the *corpus callosum,* the substance that holds together—and forms a crucial link between—the two hemispheres of the brain. The cure is radical, as is all brain surgery, but on the whole completely successful. Except, that is, for some very unusual side effects.

Into which we shall go later; my own epilepsy has been cured in this way. But, to return, the problem now is that all the beginnings are very apt, very apt indeed. Three of them though: three routes leading God knows where. And then, endings, too, are equally important, for—really—what I'm after is the truth. Or even TRUTH. A very elusive character. As elusive as bloody Kramer, sod him.

My preoccupation with truth arises from the division of my *corpus callosum* and explains why I am reading this book called *Truth, Falsehood and Philosophy.* I open at random. Chapter Two: Expressing Beliefs in Sentences. "Beliefs are hard to study directly and many sentences do not naturally state beliefs. . . ." My eyes dart impatiently down the page: ". . . although truth does *not* have degrees it *does* have many borderline cases." At last something pertinent. For someone with my unique problems these donnish evasions and qualifications are incredibly frustrating. So, "truth has borderline cases." Good. I'm glad to find the academics admit this much, especially as since my operation the whole world has become a borderline case for me.

Kramer was at school with me. To be candid I admired him greatly and he casually exploited my admiration. In fact you could say that I loved Kramer—in a brotherly sort of way—to such an extent that, had he bothered to ask, I would have laid down my life for him. It sounds absurd to admit this now, but there was something almost noble about Kramer's disregard for everyone except himself. You know these selfish people whose selfishness seems quite reasonable—admirable, really, in its refusal to compromise. Kramer was like that: intelligent, mysterious and self-absorbed.

We were at university together for a while, but he was scandalously sent down and went off to America, where he duly made something of a name for himself as a sort of hoodlum art critic, a cultural vigilante with no respect for reputations. I often saw shadowy photographs of him in fashionable glossy magazines, and it was in one of them that I learned of his marriage—after ten years of rampant bachelorhood—to one Joan Aslinger, heiress to a West Coast fast-food chain.

Kramer and I had grown to become close friends of a sort and I continued to write to him regularly. I'm happy to report that he kept in touch: the odd letter, kitsch postcards from Hammamet or Tijuana. He used to come and stay as well—with his current girl-friend, whoever that might be—in my quiet Devon cottage for a boisterous weekend every two years or so.

I remember he was surprisingly solicitous when he heard about my operation and in an uncharacteristic gesture of largesse sent a hundred white roses to the clinic where I was convalescing. He promised shortly to visit me with his new wife, Joan.

It was during one of my periodic sojourns in the sanatorium that I experienced the particularly acute and destructive epileptic attack that prompted the doctors to recommend the severing of my *corpus callosum*. The operation was a complete success. I remember only waking up as bald as a football, with a thin, livid stripe of lacing running fore and aft along my skull.

The surgeon—a Mr. Berkeley, a genial elderly Irishman—did mention the unusual side effects I would have as a result of the *coupage* but dismissed them with a benign smile as being "metaphysical" in character and quite unlikely to impair the quality of my daily life. Foolishly, I accepted his assurances.

Kramer and his wife came to stay as promised. Joan was a fairly attractive girl; she had delightful honey-blond hair—always so clean—bright blue eyes and a loose, generous mouth. She chatted and laughed in what was clearly an attempt at sophisticated animation, but it was immediately obvious to me that she was hopelessly neurotic and quite unsuited to be Kramer's wife. When they were together the tension that crackled between them was unbearable. On the first night they stayed, I overheard a savage, teeth-clenched row in the guest bedroom.

It was the effect on Kramer that I found most depressing. He was drawn and cowed, like a cornered, beaten man. His brilliant wit was reduced to glum monosyllables or fervent contradictions of any opinion Joan ventured to express. Irritation and despair were lodged in every feature of his face.

It didn't surprise me greatly when, three strained days later, Kramer announced that he had to go to London on business and Joan and I found ourselves with a lot of time on our hands. She tried hard, I have to admit, but I found her tedious and dull, as most obsessively introspective people tend to be. She came slightly more alive when she drank, which was frequently, and our prandial lunch-time session swiftly advanced to elevenses.

I soon got the full story of Kramer's constant bastardy, of course: a tearful finger-knotting account,

leaden with self-pity, that went on well into the night.
Other women apparently, from the word go. Things
had become dramatically worse because now, it seemed,
there was one in particular: one Erica—said with much
venom—an old flame. As Erica's description emerged,
I realised to my surprise that I knew her. She had figured in two of Kramer's visits before his marriage to
Joan. Erica was a tall, intelligent redhead, strong-shouldered and of arresting appearance and with a calm and
confident personality. I had liked her a lot. Naturally I
didn't tell any of this to Joan, whom—as Kramer pre-
dictably rang from London announcing successive de-
lays—I was beginning to find increasingly tiresome; she
was getting on my nerves.

Take her reaction to my own particular case, for example. When I explained my unique problems caused
by the side effects of my operation, she didn't believe
me. She laughed, said I must be joking, claimed that
such things could never happen. I admitted such cases
were exceptionally rare but affirmed it as documented
medical fact.

I now know, thanks to this book I'm reading, the correct academic term for my "ailment." I am a "bizarre
situation." Reading on, I find this conclusion: "Our
language is not sufficiently articulated to cope with such
rare and unusual circumstances. Many philosophers and
logicians are deeply unhappy about 'bizarre situations.' " So, even the philosophers have to admit it. In
my case there is no hope of ever reaching the truth. I
find the concession reassuring somehow—but I still feel
that I have to see Kramer again.

Indeed, my condition is truly bizarre. Since the link
between my cerebral hemispheres was severed, my brain
now functions as two discrete halves. The only bodily
function that this effects is perception, and the essence

of the problem is this. If I see, for example, a cat in my *left*-side area of vision and I am asked to write down what I have seen with my *right* hand—I am right-handed—I cannot. I cannot write down what I have seen because the right half of my brain no longer registers what occurred in my left-hand area of vision. This is because the hemispherical division in your brain extends, so to speak, the length of your body. Right hemisphere controls right side; left hemisphere, left side. Normally the information from both sides has free passage from one hemisphere to the other—linking the two halves into one unified whole. But now that this route— the *corpus callosum*—has gone, only *half* my brain has seen the cat. The right hemisphere knows nothing about it, so it can hardly tell my right hand what to note down.

This is what the surgeon meant by "metaphysical" side effects, and he was right to say my day-to-day existence would be untroubled by them, but consider the radical consequences of this on my phenomenological world. It is now nothing but a sequence of *half*-truths. What, for me, is really true? How can I be sure if something that happens in my left-side area of vision really took place, if in one half of my body there is *absolutely no record of it ever having occurred*?

I spend befuddled hours wrestling with these arcane epistemological riddles. Doubt is underwritten; it comes to occupy a superior position to truth and falsehood. I am a genuine, physiologically real sceptic—medically consigned to this fate by the surgeon's knife. Uncertainty is the only thing I can really be sure of.

You see what this means, of course. In my world, truth is exactly what I want to believe.

I came to this book hoping for some sort of guidance, but it can only bumble on about the "insufficient articulation of our language," which is absolutely no help at all, however accurate it may be. For example, the door of this café I'm sitting in is on my left-hand side. I clearly see in my left field of vision a tall woman in black come through it and advance towards the bar. I take a pen from my pocket and intend to write down what I saw in the margin of my book. I say to myself: "Write down what you saw coming through the door." I cannot do it, of course. As far as the right-hand side of my body is concerned, the lady in black does not exist. So which hemisphere of my brain do I trust, then? Which version of the truth do I accept: lady or no lady?

They are both true as far as I am concerned, and whatever I decide, one half of my body will back my judgement to the death.

Of course there is a simple way out: I can turn round, bring her into my right field of vision, firmly establish her existence. But that's entirely up to me. Oh, yes. Unlike the rest of you, verification is a gift I can bestow or withdraw at will.

I turn. I see her. She is tall, with curly reddish auburn hair. Our eyes meet, part, meet again. Recognition flares. It is Erica.

It was I who discovered Joan's body on the floor of the guest bedroom. (One shot: my father's old Smith & Wesson pressed against her soft palate. I use the revolver—fully licensed of course—to blast at the rooks that sometimes wheel and caw round the house. Indeed, Joan and I spent a tipsy afternoon engaged in this sport. I couldn't have known. . . .)

Kramer was still in London. I had gone out to a dinner party, leaving Joan curled up with a whisky bottle—she had muttered something about a migraine. Naturally, I phoned the police at once.

Kramer arrived on the first train from London the next morning, numbed and shattered by the news.

At the inquest—a formality—it came out that Joan had attempted suicide a few months earlier and Kramer admitted to the rockiness of their marriage. He stayed with me until it was all over. They were stressful, edgy days. Kramer was taciturn and preoccupied, which under the circumstances wasn't surprising. He did tell me, though, that he hadn't been continually in London but in fact had spent some days in Paris with Erica where some sort of emotional crisis had ensued. He had only been back thirty-six hours when the police phoned his London hotel with the news of Joan's death.

And now Erica herself sits opposite me. Her face has very little make-up on and she looks tense and worried. After the initial pleasantries we both blurt out, "What are you doing here?" and both realise simultaneously that we are here for the same reason. Looking for Kramer.

When Kramer left after the inquest he told me he was going to Paris to re-join Erica and make a film on De Chirico for French TV. Apparently unperturbed he had continued to sleep in the guest bedroom, but it was several days before I could bring myself to go in and clean it out. In the waste-paper basket I found several magazines, a map of Paris, a crumpled napkin from the Bar Cercle with the message, "Monday, Rue Christine" scrawled on it and, to my alarm and intense consternation, a semi-transparent credit card receipt slip from a filling station on the M4 at a place no more than an hour's drive from the house. This unsettled me. As far as I knew, Kramer had no car. And, what was more disturbing, the date on the receipt slip was the same as the night Joan died.

***

Erica is distinctly on edge. She says she has arranged to meet Kramer here tonight, as she has something to tell him. She picks at her lower lip distractedly.

"But anyway," she says with vague annoyance, "what do you want him for?"

I shrug my shoulders. "I have to see him as well," I say. "There's something I have to clear up."

"What is it?"

I almost tell her. I almost say, I want the truth. I want to know if he killed his wife. If he hired a car, drove to the house, found her alone and insensibly drunk, typed the note, put the pistol in her lolling mouth and blew the top of her head off.

But I don't. I say it's just a personal matter.

There is a pause in our conversation. I say to Erica, who nervously lights a cigarette, "Look, I think I should talk to him first."

"No!" she replies instantly. "I must speak to him." Speak to him about what? I wonder. It irritates me. Is Kramer to be hounded perpetually by these neurotic harpies? What has the man done to deserve this?

We see Kramer at the same time as he sees us. He strides over to our table. He stares angrily at me.

"What the hell are you doing here?" he demands in tones of real astonishment.

"I'm sorry," I say, nervousness making my voice tremble. "But I have to speak to you." It's like being back at school.

Erica crushes out her cigarette and jumps to her feet. I can see she is blinking back tears.

"I have news for you," she says, fighting to keep her voice strong. "Important news."

Kramer grips her by the elbows. "Come back," he says softly, pleadingly.

I am impatient with whatever lovelorn drama it is that

they are enacting, and also obscurely angered by this demeaning display of reliance. Raising my voice I flourish the credit card receipt. "Kramer," I say. "I want to know about this."

He ignores me. He does not take his eyes from Erica. "Erica, please," he entreats.

She lowers her head and looks down at her shaking hands.

"No," she says desperately. "I can't. I'm marrying Jean-Louis. I said I would tell you tonight. Please let me go." She shakes herself free of his arms and brushes past him, out into the night. I am glad to see her go.

I have never seen a man look so abject. Kramer stands with his head bowed in defeat, his jaw muscles bulging, his eyes fixed—as if he's just witnessed some dreadful atrocity. I despise him like this, so impoverished and vulnerable, nothing like the Kramer I knew.

I lean forward. "Kramer," I say softly, confidingly. "You can tell me now. You did it, didn't you? You came back that night while I was away." I spread the slip of transparent paper on the table. "You see I have the facts here." I keep my voice low. "But don't worry, it's between you and me. I just need to know the truth."

Kramer sits down unsteadily. He examines the receipt. Then he looks up at me as if I'm quite mad.

"Of course I came back," he whispers bitterly. "I drove back that night to tell Joan I was leaving her, that I wanted Erica." He shakes his head in grim irony. "Instead I saw everything. From the garden. I saw you sitting in your study. You had a kind of bandage round your head. It covered one eye." He points to my right eye. "You were typing with one hand. Your left hand. You only used one hand. All the time. I saw you take the gun from the drawer with your left hand." He paused. "I knew what you were going to do. I didn't want to stop you." He stands up. "You are a sick man," he says, "with your sick worries. You can delude yourself perhaps, but nobody else." He looks at me as if he can taste vomit in his mouth. "I stood there and listened for the shot. I went along with the game. I share the guilt. But it was you who did it." He turns and walks out of the café.

KRAMER IS LYING. It is a lie. The sort of mad impossible fantastic lie a desperate man would dream up. I know he is lying because I know the truth. It's locked in my brain. It is inviolate. I have my body's authority for it.

Still, there is a problem now with this lie he's set loose. Mendacity is a tenacious beast. If it's not nipped in the bud it's soon indistinguishable from the truth. I told him he didn't need to worry. But now . . .

He is bound to return to this melancholy bar before long. I know the banal nostalgia of such disappointed men—haunting the sites of their defeats—and the powerful impulses of unrequited love. I will have to see Kramer again; sort things out once and for all.

I signal the waiter for my bill. As I close my book a sentence at the bottom of the page catches my eye:

> Many logicians and philosophers are deeply unhappy about bizarre situations.

A curse on them all, I say.

Gifts

We land in Nice. Pan Am. I go through customs without much trouble and stand around the arrivals hall wondering what to do next—if there's a bus into town; whether I should get a taxi. I see a man—black hair, white face, blue suit—looking curiously at me. I decide to ignore him.

He comes over, though.

"Tupperware?" he asks unctuously. He pronounces it *tooperwère.*

"Sorry?" I say.

"Ah, English," he says with some satisfaction, as if he's done something clever. "Mr. Simpson." He picks up my suitcase. It's heavier than he expects. He has tinted spectacles and his black hair is getting thin at the front. He looks about forty.

"No," I say. I tell him my name.

He puts my suitcase down. He looks around the arrivals hall at the few remaining passengers. I am the only one not being met.

"*Merde,*" he swears softly. He shrugs his shoulders. "Do you want a ride into town?"

We go outside to his car. It's a big Citroën. The back is filled with plastic beakers, freezer boxes, salad crispers and such like. He puts my case in the boot. He shovels stacks of pamphlets off the front seat before he lets me into his car. He explains that he has been sent to meet his English opposite number from Tupperware UK. He says he assumed I was English from my clothes. In fact, he goes on to claim that he can guess any European's nationality from the kind of clothes he or she is wearing. I ask him if he can distinguish Norwegians from Danes and for some reason he seems to find this very funny.

We drive off smartly, following the signs for Nice *centre ville*. I can't think of anything to say, as my French isn't good enough and somehow I don't like the idea of talking to this man in English. He sits very close to the steering-wheel and whistles softly through his teeth, occasionally raising one hand in rebuke at any car that cuts in too abruptly on him. He asks me, in French, how old I am and I tell him I'm eighteen. He says I look older than that.

After a while he reaches into the glove compartment and takes out some photographs. He passes them over to me.

"You like?" he says in English.

They are pictures of him on a beach standing by some rocks. He is absolutely naked. He looks in good shape for a forty-year-old man. In one picture I see he's squatting down and some trick of the sun and shadow makes his cock seem enormously long.

"Very nice," I say, handing them back, "but *non merci*."

He drops me in the middle of the Promenade des Anglais. We shake hands and he drives off. I stand for a while looking down on the small strip of pebble beach. It's January and the beach is empty. The sky is packed with grey clouds and the sea looks an unpleasant blue-green. For some reason I was expecting sunshine and parasols. I let my eyes follow the gentle curve of the Baie des Anges. I start at the airport and travel along the sweep of the coast. The palm trees, the neat little Los Angeleno-style hotels with their clipped poplars and fancy wrought-ironwork, along past the first of the apartment blocks, blind and drab with their shutters firmly down, past the Negresco with its pink sugary domes, past the Palais de la Méditerranée, along over the old Port, completing the slow arc at the promontory of Cap St.-Jean, surmounted by its impossible villa. I see the ferry from Corsica steaming gamely into harbour. I stand looking for a while until I begin to feel a bit cold.

It's Sunday so I can't enrol for my courses at the university until the next day. I carry my case across the Promenade des Anglais, go up one street and book into the first hotel I see. It's called the Hotel Astoria. I go down some steps into a dim foyer. An old man gives me a room.

I sit in my room reading for most of the evening. At about half past nine I go out for a coffee. Coming back to the hotel I notice several young girls standing in front of brightly lit shop windows in the Rue de France. Despite the time of year they are wearing boots and hot pants. They all carry umbrellas (unopened) and swing bunches of keys. I walk past them two or three times but they don't pay much attention. I observe that some of them are astoundingly pretty. Every now and then a car stops, there is a brief conversation, and one of the girls gets in and is driven away.

Later that night as I am sitting on my bed reading, there is a knock on my door. It turns out to be the fat daughter of the hotel manager. He has told her I am English and she asks if I will help her do a translation that she's been set for homework.

I enrol at the university. This takes place at a building called the Centre Universitaire Méditerranéen or CUM as it's generally known (the French pronounce it "cume"). The building is on the Promenade des Anglais and looks like a small, exclusive art gallery. Inside there is a huge lecture room with a dull mythological mural on three walls. This morning I am the first to arrive and there is a hushed marmoreal stillness in the place. In a small office I enrol and pay my fees. I decide to postpone my first class until the next day as I have to find somewhere to live. A secretary gives me a list of addresses where I can rent a room. I look for the cheapest. Mme. D'Amico, it says at the bottom of the list, 4 Rue Dante. I like the address.

As I leave the Centre I see some of my fellow students for the first time. They all seem to be foreign—in the sense that not many are French. I notice a tall American girl surrounded by chattering Nigerians. There are some Arabs. Some very blond girls whom I take to be Scandinavian. Soon the capacious marble-floored entrance hall begins to fill up as more and more people arrive for their classes. I hear the pop-pop of a motor bike in the small courtyard at the front. Two young guys with long hair come in talking English. Everyone seems happy and friendly. I leave.

Rue Dante is not far from the Centre. Number four is a tall old apartment block with bleached shutters and crumbling stonework. On the ground floor is a café. CAVE DANTE it says in plastic letters. I ask the concierge for Mme. D'Amico and am directed up three flights of stairs to the top floor. I ring the bell, mentally running through the phrases I have prepared. *"Mme, D'Amico? Je suis étudiant anglais. Je cherche une chambre. On m'a donné votre nom au Centre Universitaire Méditerranéen."* I ring the bell again and hear vague stirrings from the flat. I sense I am being stared at through the peep-hole set in the solid wooden door. After a lengthy time of appraisal, it opens.

Mme. D'Amico is very small—well under five feet. She has a pale, thin, wrinkled face and grey hair. She is dressed in black. On her feet she is wearing carpet slippers which seem preposterously large, more suitable for a thirteen-stone man. I learn later that this is because sometimes her feet swell up like balloons. Her eyes are brown and, though a little rheumy, are bright with candid suspicion. However, she seems to understand my French and asks me to come in.

Her flat is unnervingly dark. This is because use of the electric lights is forbidden during hours of daylight. We stand in a long, gloomy hallway off which several doors lead. I sense shapes—a wardrobe, a hatstand, a chest, even what I take to be a gas cooker, but I assume my eyes are not yet accustomed to the murk. Mme. D'Amico shows me into the first room on the left. She opens shutters. I see a bed, a table, a chair, a wardrobe. The floor is made of loose red hexagonal tiles that click beneath my feet as I walk across to look out of the window. I peer down into the apartment building's central courtyard. Far below, the concierge's Alsatian is scratching itself. From my window I can see into at least five other apartments. I decide to stay here.

Turning round I observe the room's smaller details. The table is covered with a red and brown checked oilcloth on which sits a tin ashtray with suze printed on it. On one wall Mme. D'Amico has affixed two posters. One is of Mont Blanc. The other is an SNCF poster of Biarritz. The sun has faded all the bright colours to grey and blue. Biarritz looks as cold and unwelcoming as the Alps.

I am not the only lodger at Mme. D'Amico's. There is a muscle-bound taciturn engineer called Hugues. His room is separated from mine by the W.C. He is married and goes home every weekend to his wife and

family in Grenoble. Two days after I arrive, the phone
rings while I am alone in the flat. It is Hugues' wife and
she sounds nervous and excited. I somehow manage to
inform her that Hugues is out. After some moments of
incomprehension I eventually gather that it is impera-
tive for Hugues to phone her when he comes in. I say
I will give him the message. I sweat blood over that
message. I get my grammar book and dictionary out and
go through at least a dozen drafts. Finally I prop it by
the phone. It was worth the effort. Hugues is very
grateful and from that day more forthcoming, and Mme.
D'Amico makes a point of congratulating me on my
French. She seems more impressed by my error-free and
correctly accented prose than by anything else about me.
So much so that she asks me if I want to watch TV with
her tonight. I sense that this is something of a break-
through: Hugues doesn't watch her TV. But then,
maybe he has better things to do.

Almost without any exertion on my part, my days take
on a pattern. I go to the Centre in the morning and
afternoon for my courses. At lunch and in the evening
I eat at the enormous university cafeteria up by the Law
faculty. I return home, have a cup of coffee in the Cave
Dante, then pass the rest of the evening watching TV
with Mme. D'Amico and a neighbour—a fat jolly woman
to whom I have never been introduced but whose name,
I know, is Mme. Franchot.

Mme. D'Amico and Mme. Franchot sit in armchairs.
I bring a wooden chair in from the hall and sit behind
them, looking at the screen between their heads. While
the TV is on, all other source of illumination is switched
off and we sit and watch in a spectral grey light. Mme.
D'Amico reads out loud every piece of writing that appears on the screen—the titles of programmes, the entire list of credits, the names and endorsements of
products being advertised. At first I find this intensely

irritating and the persistent commentary almost insupportable. But she speaks fairly softly and after a while I get used to her voice.

We watch TV in Mme. D'Amico's bedroom. She has no sitting room as such. I think that used to be the function of my room. Hugues sleeps in what was the kitchen. He has a sink unit at the foot of his bed. Mme. D'Amico cooks in the hall (I was right: it was a cooker) and washes up in the tiny bathroom. This contains only a basin and a bidet and there are knives and forks laid out alongside toothbrushes and flannels on a glass shelf. There is no bath, which proved something of a problem to me at the outset, as I'm quite a clean person. So every two or three days I go to the municipal swimming baths at the Place Magnan. Formal, cheerless, cold, with pale-green tiles everywhere, but it stops me from smelling.

The fourth room in the flat is a dining room, though it's never used for this purpose, as this is where Mme. D'Amico works. She works for her son, who is something—a shipper, I think—in the wine trade. Her job is to attach string to a label illustrating the region the wine comes from and then to tie the completed label round the neck of a wine bottle. The room is piled high with crates of wine, which she sometimes calls on me to shift. Most days when I come back I see her sitting there, patiently tying labels round the necks of the wine bottles. It must be an incredibly boring job. I've no idea how much her son pays her but I suspect it's very little. But Mme. D'Amico is methodical and busy. She works like hell. People are always coming to take away the completed crates. I like to think she's really stinging her son.

There are lots of girls I'd like to fuck who do courses with me at the Centre. Lots. I sit there in the class with them and think about it, unable to concentrate on my studies. I've spoken to a few people but I can't as yet call any of them friends. I know a Spanish girl and an English girl but they both live outside Nice with their parents. The English girl is called Victoria and is chased all day by a Tunisian called Rida. Victoria's father was a group captain in the R.A.F. and has retired to live in Grasse. "Out to Grasse," Victoria calls it. Somehow I don't think the group captain would like Rida. Victoria is a small, bland blonde. Not very attractive at all, but Rida is determined. You've got to admire his persistence. He doesn't try anything on, is just courteous and helpful, tries to make Victoria laugh. He never leaves her side all day. I'm sure if he perseveres, his luck will turn. Victoria seems untroubled by his constant presence, but I can't see anything in Rida that would make him attractive to a girl. He is of average height, wears bright-coloured, cheap-looking clothes. His hair has a semi-negroid kink in it which he tries to hide by ruthlessly brushing it flat against his head. But his hair is too long for this style to be effective and it sticks out at the sides and the back like a helmet or an ill-fitting navy cap.

There are genuine pleasures to be derived from having a room of one's own. Sometimes at night I fling back the covers and masturbate dreamily about the girls at the Centre. There is a Swedish girl called Danni whom I like very much. She has big breasts and long white-blond hair. Is very laughing and friendly. The only trouble is that one of her legs is considerably thinner than the other. I believe she had polio when young. I think about going to bed with her and wonder if this defect would put me off.

***

My relationship with Mme. D'Amico is very formal and correct. We converse in polite phrases that would not disgrace a Victorian drawing room. She asks me, one day, to fill out a white *fiche* for the police—something, she assures me hastily, every resident must do. She notices my age on the card and raises her eyebrows in mild surprise. She says she hadn't supposed me to be so young. Then one morning, apropos of nothing, she explains why she reads everything that appears on TV. It seems that Mme. Franchot is illiterate. If Mme. D'Amico didn't relate them to her, she would never even know the names of the old films we watch nightly on Monte Carlo TV. I find I am surprisingly touched by this confidence.

One evening I go to a café with Rida after our courses and meet up with some of his Tunisian friends. They are all enrolled at one educational institution or another for the sake of the *carte d'étudiant.* They tell me it's very valuable, that they would not be allowed to stay in France if they didn't possess one. Rida, it has to be said, is one of the few who actually tries to learn something. He shares a room with a man called Ali, who is very tall and dapper. Ali wears a blazer with brass buttons which has a pseudo-English crest on the breast pocket. Ali says he bought it off a tourist. The English style is *très chic* this year. We drink some beer. Rida tells me how he and Ali recently met a Swiss girl who was hitch-hiking around Europe. They took her back to their room and kept her there. They locked her in during the day. Rida lowers his voice. *"On l'a baissé,"* he tells me conspiratorially. *"Baisser. Tu comprends?"* He says he's sure she was on drugs, as she didn't seem to mind, didn't object at all. She escaped one afternoon and stole all their stuff.

The café is small, every shiny surface lined with grease. It gets hot as the evening progresses. There is one very hard-faced blond woman who works the cash register behind the bar; otherwise we are all men. I drink too much beer. I watch the Tunisians sodomise the pinball machine, banging and humping their pelvises against the flat end. The four legs squeal their outrage angrily on the tiled floor. At the end of the evening I lend Rida and Ali twenty francs each.

Another phone call when I'm alone in the flat. It's from a doctor. He says to tell Mme. D'Amico that it is all right for her to visit her husband on Saturday. I am a little surprised. I never imagined Mme. D'Amico had a husband—because she always wears black, I suppose. I pass on the message and she explains that her husband lives in a sanatorium. He has a disease. She starts trembling and twitching all over in graphic illustration.

"Oh," I say. "Parkinson's disease."

"*Oui*," she acknowledges. "*C'est ça. Parkingsums.*"

This unsought-for participation in Mme. D'Amico's life removes another barrier. From this day on she uses my first name—always prefixed, however, by "Monsieur." "Monsieur Edward," she calls me. I begin to feel more at home.

I see that it was a misplaced act of generosity on my part to lend Rida and Ali that money as I am now beginning to run short myself. There is a postal strike in Britain which is lasting far longer than I expected. It is quite impossible to get any money out. Foolishly I expected the strike to be short-lived. I calculate that if I radically trim my budget I can last for another three weeks, or perhaps a little longer. Assuming, that is, that Rida and Ali pay me back.

***

When there is nothing worth watching on television I sit at the window of my room—with the lights off—and watch the life going on in the apartments round the courtyard. I can see Lucien, the *patron* of the Cave Dante, sitting at a table reading a newspaper. Lucien and his wife share their apartment with Lucien's brother and his wife. They all work in the café. Lucien is a gentle bald man with a high voice. His wife has a moustache and old-fashioned black-framed almond-shaped spectacles. Lucien's brother is a big hairy fellow called Jean-Louis who cooks in the café's small kitchen. His wife is a strapping blonde who reminds me vaguely of Simone Signoret. One night she didn't draw the curtains in her bedroom properly and I had quite a good view of her undressing.

I am now running so low on money that I limit myself to one cup of coffee a day. I eat apples all morning and afternoon until it is time for my solitary meal in the university restaurant up by the *fac du droit*. I wait until the end because then they give away free second helpings of rice and pasta if they have any left over. Often I am the only person in the shining well-lit hall. I sit eating bowl after bowl of rice and pasta while the floors are swabbed around me and I am gradually hemmed in by chairs being set on the tables. After that I wander around the centre of town for a while. At half nine I make my way back to the flat. The whores all come out at half nine precisely. It's quite amazing. Suddenly they're everywhere. Rue Dante, it so happens, is right in the middle of the red light district. Sometimes on my way back the girls solicit me. I laugh in a carefree manner, shrug my shoulders and tell them I'm an impoverished student. I have this fantasy that one night one of the girls will offer to do it free but so far I've had no success.

If I've saved up my cup of coffee for the evening, my day ends at the Cave Dante. I sit up at the zinc bar. Lucien knows my order by now and he sets about making up a *grande crème* as soon as I come in the door. On the top of the bar are baskets for brioches, croissants and pizza. Sometimes there are a few left over from breakfast and lunch. One night I have a handful of spare centimes and I ask Lucien how much the remaining bit of pizza costs. To my embarrassment I still don't have enough to buy it. I mutter something about not being hungry and I've changed my mind. Lucien looks at me for a moment and tells me to help myself. Now every night I go in and finish off what's left. Each time I feel a flood of maudlin sentiment for the man, but he seems uneasy when I try to express my gratitude.

One of the problems about being poor is that I can't afford to send my clothes to the "*Pressings*" any more. And Mme. D'Amico won't allow washing in the flat. Dirty shirts mount up on the back of my single chair like so many soiled antimacassars. In a corner of the wardrobe I keep dirty socks and underpants. I occasionally spray the damp heap with my aerosol deodorant as if I were some fastidious pest controller. When all my shirts are dirty I evolve a complicated rota for wearing them. The idea is that I wear them each for one day, trying to allow a week between subsequent wears in the faint hope that the delay will somehow have rendered them cleaner. At least it will take longer for them to get *really* dirty. At the weekend I surreptitiously wash a pair of socks and underpants and sneak them out of the house. I go down to an isolated part of the beach and spread them on the pebbles, where a watery February sun does a reasonable job of drying them out.

One Saturday afternoon I am sitting on the shingle beach employed in just such a way. I wonder sadly if this will be my last weekend in Nice. The postal strike wears on, I have forty-two francs and a plane ticket to London. Small breakers nudge and rearrange the pebbles at the water's edge. This afternoon the sea is filled with weed and faeces from an untreated sewage outlet a little way up the coast. Freak tides have swept the effluence into the Baie des Anges. The sun shines, but it is a cool and uncongenial day.

The thought of leaving Nice fills me with an intolerable frustration. Nice has a job to do for me, a function to fulfil and it hasn't even begun to discharge its responsibility.

I hear steps crunching on the stones, coming towards me. I look round. It is Rida with a girl I don't recognise. Frantically I stuff my washing into its plastic bag.

"*Salut,*" Rida says.

"*Ça va?*" I reply nonchalantly.

"What are you doing here?" Rida asks.

"Oh . . . nothing particular."

We exchange a few words. I look carefully at the girl. She is wearing jeans and a tie-dyed T-shirt. She has reddish blond medium-length hair and a flat freckly face. It is not unattractive though. Her eyebrows are plucked away to thin lines and her nose is small and sharp. She seems confident and relaxed. To my surprise Rida tells me she's English.

"English?" I say.

"Hi," she says. "My name's Jackie."

Rida has literally just picked her up on the Promenade. I don't know how he singles them out. I think he feels he has another Swiss girl here. He saw me sitting on the beach and told Jackie he knew an English guy he would like her to meet.

We sit around for a bit. I talk in English to Jackie. We swap backgrounds. She comes from Cheshire and has been living in Nice for the last four months. Latterly she has worked as *au pair* to a black American family. The father is a professional basketball player, one of several who play in the French leagues now that they're too old or too unfit to make the grade in the U.S.

With all this English being spoken, Rida is beginning to feel left out of it, and is impatiently throwing pebbles into the sea. However, he knows that the only way for him to get this girl is through me and so he suggests we all go to a disco. I like the sound of this because I sense by now that Jackie is not totally indifferent to me herself. She suggests we go to the Psyché, a rather exclusive disco on the Promenade des Anglais. I try to disguise my disappointment. The Psyché costs eighteen francs to get in. Then I remember that Rida still owes me twenty francs. I remind him of this fact. I'll go, I say, as long as he pays me in. Reluctantly he agrees.

We meet at nine outside the Psyché. Jackie is wearing white jeans and a scoop-necked sequinned T-shirt. She has pink shiny lipstick and her hair looks clean and freshly brushed. Rida is wearing black flared trousers and a black lacy see-through shirt unbuttoned down the front. Round his neck he has hung a heavy gold medallion. I'm glad he's changed. As we go in he touches me on the elbow.

"She's mine, okay?" he says, smiling.

"Ah-ha," I counter. "I think we should rather leave that up to Jackie, don't you?"

It is my bad luck that Jackie likes to dance what the French call *le Swing* but which the English know as the jive. I find this dance quite impossible to master. Rida, on the other hand, is something of an expert. I sit in a dark rounded alcove with a whisky and Coke (a free drink comes with the entry fee) and nervously bide my time.

Rida and Jackie come and sit down. I see small beads of sweat on Jackie's face. Rida's lace shirt is pasted to his back. We talk. A slow record comes on and I ask Jackie to dance. We sway easily to the music. Her body is hot against mine. Her clean hair is dark and damp at her temples. As if it is the most natural thing in the world I rest my lips on the base of her neck. It is damp, too, from her recent exertions in *le Swing*. Her hand moves half an inch on my back. I kiss her cheek, then her mouth. She won't use her tongue. She puts her arms round my neck. I break off for a few seconds and glance over at Rida. He is looking at us. He lights a cigarette and scrutinises its glowing end.

To my astonishment, when we sit down Jackie immediately asks Rida if he'd like to dance again, as another *Swing* record has come on. She dances with him for a while, Rida spinning her expertly round. I sip my whisky and Coke—which is fizzless by now—and wonder what Jackie is up to. She's a curious girl. When they come off the dance floor Rida announces he has to go. We express our disappointment. As he shakes my hand he gives me a wink. No hard feelings, I think he wants to say.

We go, some time later, to another club called le Go-Go. Jackie pays for me to get in. Inside we meet one of Jackie's basketballers. He is very black—almost Nubian in appearance—and unbelievably tall and thin. He is clearly something of a sporting celebrity in Nice, as we get a continuous supply of free drinks while sitting at his table. I drink a lot more whisky and Coke. Presently we are joined by three more black basketball players. I become very subdued. The blacks are friendly and extrovert. They wear a lot of very expensive-looking jewellery. Jackie dances with them all, flirts harmlessly, sits on their knees and shrieks with laughter at their jokes. All the French in the club seem to adore them. People keep coming over to our table to ask for autographs. I feel small and anaemic beside them. My personality seems lamentably pretentious and unformed. I think of my poverty, my dirty clothes, my shabby room, and I ache with an alien's self-pity, sense a refugee's angst in my bones. Then Jackie says to me, "Shall we go?" and suddenly I feel restored. We walk through quiet empty streets, the only sound the rush of water in gutters as they are automatically swilled clean. We pass a café with three tarts inside waiting for their pimp. They chatter away exuberantly.

Jackie shivers and I obligingly put my arm round her. She rests her head on my shoulder and in this fashion we awkwardly make our way to her flat. "Shh," Jackie cautions as we open the front door, "be careful you don't wake them up." I feel a rising pressure in my throat, and I wonder if the bed has squeaky springs.

We sit in the small kitchen on hard modern chairs. My buttocks feel numb and strangely cold. The fluorescent light, I'm sure, can't be flattering if its unkind effects on Jackie's pale face are anything to go by. Slowly I sense a leaden despair settle on me as we sit in this cheerless, efficient module in this expensive apartment block. *Immeuble de très grand standing,* the agent's advertisement says outside. We have kissed from time to time and I have felt both her small pointed breasts through her T-shirt. Her lips are thin and provide no soft cushion for my own. We talk now in a listless desultory fashion.

Jackie tells me she's leaving Nice next week to return to England. She wants to be a stewardess, she says, but only on domestic flights. Intercontinental ones, it seems, play hell with your complexion and menstrual cycle. Half-heartedly I offer the opinion that it might be amusing if, say, one day I should find myself flying on the very plane in which she was serving. Jackie's face becomes surprisingly animated at this notion. It seems an appropriate time to exchange addresses, which we do. I notice she spells her name "Jacqui."

This talk of parting brings with it a small cargo of emotion.

We kiss again and I slip my hand inside her T-shirt.

"No," she says gently but with redoubtable firmness.

"Please, Jackie," I say. "You're going soon." I suddenly feel very tired. "Well, at least let me see them then," I say with petulant audacity. Jackie pauses for a moment, her head cocked to one side as if she can hear someone calling her name in the distance.

"Okay then," she says. "If that's what you want. If that's all."

She stands up, pulls off her T-shirt and slips down the straps of her bra so that the cups fall free. Her breasts cast no shadow in the unreal glare of the strip light. The nipples are very small; her breasts are pale and conical and seem almost to point upward. She exposes them for five seconds or so, not looking at me, looking down at her breasts as if she's seeing them for the first time. Then she resnuggles them in her bra and puts her T-shirt back on. She makes no comment at all. It's as if she's been showing me her appendix scar.

"Look," she says unconcernedly at the door, "I'll give you a ring before I leave. Perhaps we could get together."

"Yes," I say. "Do. That would be nice."

Outside it is light. I check my watch. It's half past five. It's cold and the sky is packed with grey clouds. I walk

slowly back to Mme. D'Amico's through a sharp-fo-
cussed, scathing dawn light. Some of the cafés are open
already. Drowsy *patrons* sweep the pavements. I feel
grimy and hung over. I plod up the stairs to Mme.
D'Amico's. My room, it seems to me, has a distinct fusty,
purulent odour; the atmosphere has a stale recycled
quality, all the more acute after the uncompromising air
of the morning. I strip off my clothes. I add my un-
naturally soft shirt to the pile on the back of the chair.
I knot my socks and ball my underpants—as if to trap
their smells within their folds—and flip them into the
corner of the wardrobe. I lie naked between the sheets.
Itches start up all over my body. I finger myself exper-
imentally but I'm too tired and too sad to be bothered.

I wake up to a tremulous knocking on my door. I feel
dreadful. I squint at my watch. It's seven o'clock. I can't
have been asleep for more than an hour.

"*Monsieur Edward? C'est moi, Madame D'Amico.*"

I say come in, but no sound issues from my mouth.
I cough and run my tongue over my teeth, swallowing
energetically.

"*Entrez, Madame,*" I whisper.

Mme. D'Amico comes in. Her hair is pinned up carelessly and her old face is shiny with tears. She sits down
on the bed and immediately begins to sob quietly, her
thin shoulders shaking beneath her black cardigan.

"Oh, Madame," I say, alarmed. "What is it?" I find it
distressing to see Mme. D'Amico, normally so correct
and so formal, displaying such unabashed human
weakness. I am also—inappropriately—very aware of my
nakedness beneath the sheets.

"*C'est mon mari,*" she cries. "*Il est mort.*"

Gradually the story comes out. Apparently Monsieur
D'Amico, sufferer from Parkinson's disease, was having a final cigarette in his room in the sanatorium be-

fore the nurse came to put him to bed. He lit his cigarette and then tried to shake the match out. But his
affliction instead made the match spin from his trembling fingers and fall down the side of the plastic armchair upon which he was sitting. The chair was blazing
within seconds, Monsieur D'Amico's pyjamas and
dressing-gown caught fire, and although he managed
to wriggle himself onto the floor, his screams were not
sufficiently loud to attract the attention of the nurses
immediately. He was severely burned. The shock was
too much for his frail body and he died in the early
hours of the morning.

I try to arrange my sleepy, unresponsive senses into
some sort of order, try to summon the full extent of
my French vocabulary.

Mme. D'Amico looks at me pitifully. "Oh, Monsieur
Edward," she whimpers, her lips quivering.

"Madame," I reply helplessly. *"C'est une vraie tragé-
die."* It seems grossly inept, under the circumstances,
almost flippant, my thick early-morning tongue removing any vestige of sincerity from the words. But it seems
to mean something to Mme. D'Amico, who bows her
head and starts to cry with light, high-pitched sobs. I
reach out an arm from beneath the sheets and gently
pat her shoulder.

"There, there, Madame," I say. "It will be all right."

As I lean forward I notice that in her hands there is
a crumpled letter. Peering closer I still can't make out
the name but I do see that the stamp is British. It is
surely for me. The postal strike, I realise with a start,
must now be over. Suddenly I know that I can stay. I
think at once about Jackie and our bizarre and unsatisfactory evening. But I don't really care any more. My
spirits begin to stir and lift. I get a brief mental flash of
Monsieur D'Amico in his blazing armchair and I hear

the quiet sobs of his wife beside me. But it doesn't really impede the revelation that slowly overtakes me. People, it seems, want to give me things—for some reason known only to them. No matter what I do or how I behave, unprompted and unsought the gifts come. And they will keep on coming. Naked photos, cold pizza, their girls, their wives, their breasts to see, even their grief. I feel a growing confidence about my stay in Nice. It will be all right now, I feel sure. It will work out. I think about all the gifts that lie waiting for me. I think about the Swedish girls at the Centre. I think about spring and the days when the sun will be out. . . .

The bed continues to shudder gently from Mme. D'Amico's sobbing. I smile benignly at her bowed head.

"There, there, Madame," I say again. "Don't worry. Everything will be okay. You'll see. Everything will be fine, I promise you."

On the Yankee Station

When Lieutenant Larry Pfitz lost his Phantom on his first mission, he decided, quite spontaneously and irrationally, to blame the Vietnamese people and Arthur Lydecker, a member of his ground crew.

Pfitz was a new pilot and his face was taut as he ran through the cockpit checks before being catapulted off the heaving deck of the U.S.S. *Chester B. Halsey*. The Phantom was heavy with four clusters of 500-pound bombs, and extra poundage of pressure was demanded from the old steam catapults. Pfitz was third in line and as the *Chester B.* heeled around into the wind, the deck crew noticed the way his eyes continuously flicked from left to right at the rescue helicopters hovering alongside.

There had been a ragged jeer as Pfitz's plane dipped alarmingly on being hurled off the deck, before the straining engines thrust him up in a steep climb to join the other two members of his flight. The fourth jet was ready on the second catapult when one of the fire guards shouted and pointed up. There, in the pale-gray sky, Pfitz hung beneath his orange parachute. His plane flew on straight for a few brief seconds before tilting on one wing and curving elegantly down into the sea.

It was as well for Pfitz that, just before it smashed into the water, there was a muffled crack of explosion and a puff of smoke from the jets; otherwise the court of inquiry might have peremptorily dismissed his claim of a serious engine malfunction. Still, it left an uneasy aroma of doubt in the air. The Phantom had been new, flown over from Guam three days prior to Pfitz's arrival, and the loss of several million dollars' worth of expensive equipment for no real and pressing reason was regarded—even in this most extravagantly wasteful of wars—as a fairly serious matter. Pfitz was reprimanded for overhasty reactions, and as a measure of the captain's disapproval was assigned to fly an old Ling-Temco-Vought F-8 Crusader that was stored in the back of the below-deck hangar until a replacement Phantom arrived.

Pfitz's considerable self-esteem never recovered from this blow and his fellow pilots ribbed him unmercifully. He came to the conclusion that the loss of his Phantom was somehow symbolic of the animosity of the Vietnamese people to the American presence, and more particularly, the direct result of some gross act of carelessness on the part of his ground crew. And it was Lydecker on whom his venom alighted.

Pfitz's maintenance crew consisted of five people. There was Dawson, a huge, taciturn black; two Puerto Ricans called Pascual and Huq; Lee Otis Cooper, who came, like Pfitz, from Fayette County, Alabama; and there was Lydecker. There were good and sensible reasons for selecting Lydecker as scapegoat; Dawson was too big, Pascual and Huq too united, and Cooper—well, he was a white man. So was Lydecker, for that matter, but of a particularly inferior, Yankee city-scum sort. Lydecker came from Sturgis, New Jersey; a mean smog-mantled town that seemed to have stamped its own harsh landscape on Lydecker's body and visage. He was small, dark and thin, with pale skin and permanently red-

rimmed eyes. His face looked as if it had been com-
pressed vertically in a vise, pursing his mouth and forc-
ing his eyes close together.

Pfitz's resolute persecution came as no surprise to
Lydecker: persecution of one form or another, whether
from drunken father, bored teachers or cruel playmates,
was the abiding feature of his memories. Questions of
justice or injustice, of blame rightly apportioned, had
never carried much weight in his world. He never really
stopped to consider how unfair it was, even though he
had a good idea of who in fact was responsible. Lee Otis
had been checking the engine casings of the Phantom's
port jet the morning before Pfitz's doomed flight, and
had borrowed Lydecker's own small monkey wrench to
adjust what he thought was a loose bearing deep in the
complex mechanism. A fire drill had interrupted work
on that shift, Lydecker remembered, and he recalled Lee
Otis bolting down the inspection hatch immediately after
work was resumed. He never returned the monkey
wrench either, and, when asked for it a few days after
the accident, Lee Otis flushed momentarily before in-
forming Lydecker that he "Fuckin gave it back to you,
turdbird, so beat it, heah?"

Lydecker shrugged. Maybe he was wrong, so who gave
a shit anyway? He merely tried to keep out of Pfitz's
way as much as possible, and on occasions when he was
chewed out or put on report, accepted the screaming
flow of abuse with the practiced, hangdog, foot-shuf-
fling resentment that he knew Pfitz's injured pride demanded. Lydecker never thought about trying to change
things; experience had taught him to adapt to the
world's crazy logic. It was a hostile alien terrain of
unrelieved frustration and disappointment out there,
and this was the only method of survival he had found.
But at those times when its harsh realities inescapably

obtruded into his consciousness, he responded with a sullen, silent hatred. It was a comfort to him, his hatred; comforting because he came to realize that no matter what the world or people did to him, they couldn't regulate his emotions, couldn't stop him hating, however they tried. After particularly bad days he would exult in his hatred at night, allowing the waves of his disdain and contempt to wash through his body with the potency of some magic serum, numbing and restoring, and letting him, when the sun rose, face once again whatever the world had to offer. Recipients of his hatred had in the past included his father, and Werbel, the manager of the gas station where he had worked before he was drafted. And now there was Pfitz.

Lydecker had expected the insults, the dirty jobs and the regular appearance on report to die down after Pfitz had flown a few more missions, but if anything they intensified. Soon Lydecker came to see that the old Crusader was acting as a catalyst, a regular reminder of Pfitz's shame. Every time the Crusader was towed out amongst the Phantoms and the Skyhawks, Pfitz remembered all the details of that day: watching his new plane scythe cleanly into the waves, the hours of subjective time as he gently floated down into the sea, the rows of incredulous, grinning faces as the rescue helicopter deposited him back on board, the sly gibes and quips of his fellow officers in the messroom. And each time he climbed into the cockpit, saw the unfamiliar instrument layout and the dated mechanisms, the shame returned. And as he pulled away from the ship on a mission he imagined it brazenly echoing to the crew's gleeful laughter. And every time he took the Crusader up and landed, Lydecker was there, the man who'd caused the foul-up, weaselly shitface Lydecker, draining the fuel tanks or fitting the chocks to the wheels.

And then Pfitz would claim his cannon had misfired or the fuel-flow was unbalanced and he'd put him on report for slipshod work, or kick his narrow butt the length of the repair bay, or assign him to de-scale the afterburner all night.

For Lydecker the one benefit of the whole thing was the Crusader. His first posting had been to a Sixth Fleet carrier in the Mediterranean that still had a squadron of Crusaders in operation. He had grown familiar with the planes and had an affection for them that he did not bestow on the lean Phantoms or the dainty Skyhawks. The Crusader was a hefty rectangular machine, large for a single-seater, with the crude geometry of a bus. Its single intake was set in the nose, like a gaping mouth beneath the matte-black cone that housed the radar. It was like greeting an old friend when Pfitz's was wheeled out from storage and hoisted up to the deck. Its strong, unambiguous profile seemed to render the other planes less significant and somehow pretentious. Pfitz was loudly derogatory, complaining that she was a pig to fly and sluggish to maneuver. But then he soon discovered in it other qualities that he employed in wreaking his revenge on the population of Vietnam.

The payload of the Crusader was prodigious; its sturdy frame could carry an anthology of destructive weaponry beneath its wings. Pfitz was highly satisfied with this aspect, soon indifferent to the absence of computer technology that precluded his carrying laser or guided bombs like the Phantoms. And he was never happier than when he supervised his crew as they bolted the finless, cigar-shaped canisters of napalm to the underwing pylons. Pascual overheard him talking about a request he'd made to be excused from carrying all other bomb loads and how he'd voluntarily restricted himself to napalm. He started to refer to his aircraft as the Rose

Train and had Huq, who was something of an artist, paint this below his cockpit.

"It's like roses in the jungle, man," he would crow on returning from a mission. "You see them cans tumblin' and *whoomph*—it's like a fuckin' great flower bloomin' in the trees. Wham, pink an' orange roses. Beautiful, man, just beautiful." He made Huq keep a tally of missions by painting a red rose beneath the cockpit sill.

Lydecker thought Pfitz had gone mad, and so did many of the other pilots. Napalm had to be delivered from low level, making the plane vulnerable to ground fire. With half a dozen canisters wobbling like overripe fruit beneath your wings, you could be transformed into a comet of blazing petroleum jelly with one lucky shot. Lydecker sometimes thought about this as he patched bullet holes in the wings and tail.

Often at night Lydecker would leave the brightly lit crew quarters, where the air was thick with smoke, and bored sailors played cards or told obscene stories, and wander up to the dark cavern of the main hangar below the deck where the atmosphere had a tranquil metallic chill and the smell of oil and engine coolant clung to the air. He would go over to the Crusader, ponderously low-slung on its curious trolley undercarriage which jutted like spavined legs from the fuselage belly, and run his hands over the scarred and chipped aluminum, his fingers tracing and caressing the lines of rivet heads. Like the halted, bullied schoolchild who tinkers with his bike all day, Lydecker enjoyed the mute presence of his plane. It was like some gigantic familiar toy, stored in a cupboard with its wings folded and canopy up. He knew every square inch of the plane, from its gaping intake to the scorched jet at the rear. He had clambered all over its body, fueling and rearming it, riveting patches of aluminum alloy over the puckered

ulcers caused by random bullets. He had climbed into
the dark ventral recesses of the undercarriage bay,
checking the hydraulic system, and had inched along
its ribbed length replacing frayed control wires and re-
aligning the armor plate. And he found himself, like
an anxious mother, fretting for its return after long
missions to Laos or Haiphong.

The war was a distant affair to the men on the "Yankee
Station" in the South China Sea. Just a green haze on
the horizon sometimes. Even for the pilots who flew
above it, dumping tons of high explosive on the jungle,
the war and the enemy remained abstract and remote.
To them it was a dangerous, demanding job and only
Pfitz openly expressed the requisite warlike antago-
nism; only he seemed to be exulted by the regular missions and the crop of red roses that grew on the side
of the plane.

   Then one late afternoon a seabird was sucked into
the intake as the Crusader came in to land. The thump
made Pfitz veer up and away to make his approach
again. This caused a lot of hilarity among the deck crew
and when Pfitz had landed safely someone shouted,
"Hey! Why din't ya eject, Pfitz?" There was no real
danger, as, set about five feet down the intake vent, there
was a fine wire mesh that protected the delicate com-
pressor fans of the engine from such incidents.

   Lydecker wheeled the light ladder against the fuselage as soon as the plane was towed to its bay on the
deck. Pfitz took off his helmet, sweat shining in his crew-
cut hair, his beefy face red with anger. As he climbed
down, Lydecker stepped back from the ladder and
looked away, but Pfitz grabbed him by the arm, fingers
biting cruelly into his bicep.

   "Fuckin' bumpy landing again, you fuckin' shithead

creep. How many times I told you to get those tire pressures reduced? You're on fuckin' report."

That night Lydecker abandoned the letter he was trying to write to a movie usherette he had known in Sturgis and made his way up to the hangar. He roved around the familiar contours of the plane, noting with a surge of anger the bulge of the fat soft tires on the steel floor. His brain hummed with an almost palpable hatred for Pfitz. His hands were raw and astringent from an evening spent cleaning latrines with coarse scouring powder as a result of his having been placed on report. He leaned up against the side of the Crusader and rested his hot cheek on the cool metal, his eyes blank and tearless, yet his mouth uncontrollably twisted in a rictus of sadness and utter frustration with his life. He forced himself to think of something else. He thought of the plane and the bird it had engulfed, how his heart had leaped in panic as the plane had jerked from its approach run. Without thinking he peered into the maw of the intake. In the gloom he could make out the detritus of feathers and expressed flesh stuck to the fine grille. He climbed into the intake, easily adapting the posture of his body to the narrowing curves of the interior, and began to pick the feathers and bones away from the wire mesh. He felt his spine molded against the curve of polished metal and sensed all about him the complex terminals of controls and cables running from the cockpit above his head. The only sound was the noise of his breathing and the quiet pinging of his nails on the wires as he plucked the trapped feathers away.

When he heard the voices he suddenly realized he did not know how long he'd been hunched in the throat of the plane. With a chill of alarm he recognized Pfitz's oddly high laugh among them and hastily clambered out of the intake. He saw three officers sauntering toward the Crusader down the aisle of parked aircraft. Momentarily distracted, he tried to slip around the plane out of sight but Pfitz had seen him and ran forward.

"Hey! You there, sailor, stop!"

Lydecker stood at attention, his face red with embarrassment, as if his mother had discovered him having sex or masturbating. As Pfitz approached, the shame dissipated and fear suddenly gripped like a hand at his heart.

"Lydecker! This is off limits to you, man." Pfitz was enraged; he clutched a beer can in his fist. "What're you fuckin' doing here, jerk-off?"

The other two officers stood back grinning. Pfitz was aware of their amused observation.

Lydecker held out his hand, showing the ball of fluff and feathers by way of explanation.

"Uh, I was just clearing the intake, sir. The bird? You know, when you landed this afternoon . . . ?"

The two officers snorted with laughter. Pfitz's eyes widened in fury. He cuffed at the feathers, and the bundle exploded into a cloud of swooping fluff.

"Hey, Larry," one of the officers guffawed, "it's a fuckin' souvenir, man."

Pfitz struck out blindly at Lydecker, punching him in the chest. Lydecker staggered backward. Pfitz's voice rose to a shriek.

"You're fuckin' finished, you fuckin' dipshit asshole! Get outa here an' don't come back or I'm gonna dump a giant shit on you, boy!"

Pfitz held the beer can up threateningly. Lydecker backed down the row of planes. Helpless with laughter, the two officers tried to restrain Pfitz.

"You're getting transferred off of my crew. You ain't gonna mess around with me anymore, you bastard. Now git out!" His face rigid with fury, Pfitz hurled the half-full beer can at the retreating Lydecker. It glanced off his forehead and went ringing along the steel deck. Lydecker turned and fled, only to slip on a patch of oil. He skidded to the ground, careening into the nose wheel of a Skyhawk. The beer can rested against the tire. All Lydecker could hear was laughter—Pfitz's harsh, triumphant laughter. He picked up the beer can, paused for an instant, then got to his feet and limped off, the can clutched to his chest with both hands.

Pfitz had Lydecker transferred from aircraft crew to catapult maintenance, one of the worst details on the ship. It meant hours on the exposed bow of the carrier as it steamed full speed into the wind for a mission launch. Lydecker's new job was to shackle the planes on to the towing block that protruded from the indented track of the catapult. He wore a huge goggled helmet with bulging ear protectors that made him look like some insect-headed alien or demented astronaut. It was a cheerless, companionless job. The rush of wind made his bright nylon coveralls crack like a pennant in a hurricane, and conversation of any kind was impossible due to the shattering roar of jet engines driven at full thrust. As the plane was moved into take-off position, Lydecker would run forward with the cumbersome steel-cable towing strop. He would secure each end of the strop to pinions in the undercarriage bay or just below the leading edge of the wings, and slip the middle over the angled blade of the towing block. He then darted out from beneath the plane, giving a thumbs-up to the catapult officer. If everything was in order the officer held five fingers up to the pilot of the plane, who saluted his acknowledgment. Then, like some ardent coach cheering on his team, the catapult officer dropped to one knee, swept his arm forward, and a seaman on a catwalk across the deck pressed the launch button. The catapult would be released, hurling the plane, on full afterburn, along the narrow expanse of deck and into the air. The cable, too, would be flung out ahead of the carrier, dropping away from the climbing plane to splash forlornly into the sea in a tiny flurry of spray. The next plane was then towed into the take-off position, ghostly wreaths of steam hissing from the length of the catapult track.

Some strange impulse made Lydecker keep the beer can Pfitz had thrown at him. It stood on a small shelf above his bunk beside his electric razor and a creased Polaroid snapshot of the movie usherette. For a week after the incident he had worn adhesive tape on his forehead; then the scab had sloughed off, leaving a paler stripe on his already pale skin. Lydecker found that he unconsciously kept touching the thin scar, repeatedly running his forefinger over it, as if he had to keep reminding himself of its presence, like a teenager with his first moustache.

Denied the satisfaction of working on a plane, Lydecker's life became one of routine mindless boredom. There were long periods of inactivity or futile chores. There was the deadening monotony of the catapult maintenance crew; the endless scurrying beneath screaming jets with the heavy cable, the grease thick on his gloves as he fought with recalcitrant pinions. Sometimes the frequent malfunctioning of the *Chester B.*'s old steam catapult brought tedious afternoons of stripping the mechanism down, searching for faults and elusive defects. The pressure that was required to fling tons of lethal weaponry into the air caused valves to blow back, bearings to jam and gauges to crack and leak. There were many accidents. Planes, given insufficient lift from the catapult, belly-landing in the sea; a tardily raised blast deflector had caused a parked helicopter to be flipped overboard; combat-dazed pilots had misjudged their landings and ploughed off the end of the carrier. Once a deck-tractor had momentarily stuck in reverse and backed a Skyhawk into the ocean—just like kicking a pebble off a dock. Throughout this time Lydecker appeased his tired and numb body by hating Pfitz. The man came to obsess him. His throat would be thick with emotion and fury as he forced the launching cable onto the Crusader's grips. Sometimes he would wander over to the plane when the crew were working on it, but he was invariably met with insults and told to stay away. Slowly he came to feel that Pfitz had deliberately set out to deprive his life of the little meaning and satisfaction it had, and for some reason the only solace he found, the only way he knew of combating this emptiness, was to replace it with his hatred. The emotion gave his life a structure of sorts; it became something he could rely on, constant and unwavering, like a picture he had once seen of Saint Paul's cathedral in the London blitz. Lydecker's hatred was a familiar comfort; it had done able service from his earliest days. It had sustained him as he had lain in bed and listened to his father batter his frail mother in a frenzy of crapulous rage. It had provided support when Werbel took him off cars and put him on the pumps and had then restricted him to cleaning the rest rooms and sweeping the concrete apron. As he had freed plugged drains or picked sodden cigar butts from chill pools of oil, listening to the laughter and banter of the mechanics in the warm garage, all that had kept his mind from tilting over into twitching insanity was his passionate hatred. It was this and the knowledge that no matter what Werbel made him do, no matter how he was debased by him, the hate lived on—secretly firing and fueling his spirit. He was grateful to the Navy for allowing the hate to subside for a while. He still had no friends, was still one of the few despised and ignored that figure in any large company, but his ability with machinery was recognized and his self-esteem inched up from ground zero. He found his reward in the perfect roar of an engine, the smooth retraction of an under-carriage, or the clean function of an aileron. Never having asked for much, he needed nothing more, and his life reached a plateau of tolerance which was as close as he'd come to happiness. Until Pfitz had lost his Phantom.

Working away from Pfitz's immediate sphere of influence, Lydecker became more aware of the man's other obsession. Pfitz's fascination with napalm was the subject of bemused reflection among the members of the catapult maintenance crew. "Hell, there goes Fireball Pfitz," one of them would remark, and there would ensue some discussion about the "poor fuckin' gooks." Lydecker didn't pay much attention at first. He had never been to Vietnam, even though he'd been on the Yankee Station for four months. The fleet made an endless patrol, usually just over the horizon from the coast, rarely steaming into sight unless cruisers or destroyers were called to bring their large guns into play. But gradually Lydecker came to see that Pfitz hated Vietnam as much as he loathed Lydecker himself; and he felt an involuntary sympathy start up in his body as Pfitz lovingly recounted, to the wide-mouthed audience of his ground crew, the devastation eight canisters of napalm had wrought in a straw village. The Rose Train climbed the gradients into the sky weighted with seething latent fire like some modern archangelic predator. Lydecker would watch it go, his head a confused muddle of thoughts and sensations.

And each night, exhausted, he would gaze at the slightly buckled beer can as if it were some icon or idol of his hate. In the distorted planes of its surface he seemed to see a vague metallic template of Pfitz's bullish features. He would stroke the scar on his forehead and think about Pfitz and the men he had known like him—his father and Werbel—and the intensity of his hatred brought his flesh up in goose pimples. He would clutch the sides of his bunk and screw his eyes tight shut as if in the grip of an acute migraine attack. Men like that shouldn't be allowed to go about unhindered, he would think distractedly; something should be done to them.

Then one day Pfitz had an engine cut out as Lydecker was shackling the expendable wire bridle to the nose wheel of the Crusader. The air vibrated with the idling jets of planes waiting in line and the hot gases of the exhausts made the crowded deck of the carrier shimmer and dance in the haze. Pfitz had to be towed off line and there was some delay as Lydecker fought to free the cable from the stiff nose-wheel clamps. Pfitz had raised his cockpit canopy and as Lydecker stood up, the cable finally released, he saw Pfitz's purple enraged face screaming inaudible obscenities at him through arcs of spittle. It was as if Lydecker had been responsible for the cutout, as if his particular touch on the nose wheel had mysteriously spooked the functioning of the jet. And in the waves of Pfitz's anger, Lydecker was disturbed by the sudden realization that Pfitz was a hater, too; that, like him, he needed his hate, needed his malice to beat the world.

That evening Lydecker applied for some long-overdue shore leave. The bizarre feeling of kinship had unsettled him. It appeared that Pfitz's plane would be out of action for a week, and now—more than ever—Lydecker didn't want to be around.

Lydecker was granted five days and opted for Sai-

gon. He passed nearly all of his time in a Tu-Do bar
brothel, methodically working his way through the nine
girls who serviced the clients. Out at the back of the bar
there were three lean-to-cabins with rickety iron beds.
Lydecker spent the day drinking beer and every now
and then would stagger up to one of the girls—comic-
book whores with thickly mascara-ed eyes, miniskirts and
padded bras—and lurch outside to a cabin.

It was only on the third day that he noticed the young,
thin-shouldered girl who wiped and cleared the tables
and periodically swept out the cabins. She was quiet and
withdrawn and had slightly buck teeth. Unlike the others, she wore an ao-dai and a thigh-length chemise. Her
status in the bar was indeterminate. He never saw her
with G.I.'s and she never used the cabins. Sometimes
she would go out to the back or into the toilets, but only
with civilians or the occasional Vietnamese soldier, only
spending the briefest time—about two minutes—away
from her chores. She did not pout, flirt or posture like
the other girls and never wore their cheap Western
clothes. Yet for all her quiet dignity and restraint, she
was the lowest creature in the bar. A quick-time girl—
lower than the pimps and shoeshine boys, lower even
than the many cats and stray dogs that nosed around
and were temporarily adopted and spoiled by the
American servicemen. Why is she doing this? Lydecker
found himself asking. What was it about her that kept
her in this whores' city, so calmly accepting the shitty
jobs and compliantly carrying out the spurious sex acts
demanded of her? The paradox enraged and excited
him and the girl gradually took a hold on his mind. Not
having noticed her at first, he now seemed to see her
everywhere. She hovered around the perimeter of his
vision: taking the empty bottles from his table, slipping
from a cabin as he entered, mopping up pools of vomit

in the men's room. He discovered a disproportionate irritation in this, and despite himself swore and shouted at her if she approached. Strengthened by his uniform in this city of obsequious servants, he befriended other servicemen who used the bar and in his noontide drunkenness wove obscene stories around the thin girl, flashing his eyes in her direction as he joined in the raucous guffaws.

She paid no attention to him, her frail body moving among the tables, her straight, shiny hair framing her face.

At night, Lydecker tossed in his bed and found his thoughts turning again and again to the thin girl. He stayed away from the bar a whole day before crashing in late at night in a beer haze to seek her out. He found her in the corridor that led out to the cabins at the back, her arms full of dirty sheets. Lydecker bore down on her, maddened by her inscrutability and at the same time potently aroused. He wrenched the sheets from her hands and forced her against the wall, drunkenly nuzzling her neck.

She made no move to resist him. He gazed into her eyes.

"Whassa fuckin' matter with you? Damn you," he implored slurringly, "whyncha like the others? No-good chicken-shit . . ." His voice tailed off into a wet, whispering pant. He looked at her and saw why she wasn't like the others. Beneath the stretched oblique lids her brown eyes stared out defiantly in candid, unalloyed hate.

Lydecker stepped back, suddenly dismayed and shocked. "Ach, no-good fuckin' . . ." he grunted to himself and staggered off down the passage. The girl stood there, a grubby snowdrift of soiled sheets around her ankles, and watched him go.

During his last day of leave Lydecker took three
cheery whores to bed. They giggled when he stared into
their eyes.

"You like G.I.?" he would ask uncertainly.

"Sure, you number one," they would smile. "U.S.
number one."

So, no hooker fell in love with her John, Lydecker
reasoned, but where did that little bit of skinny ass get
the right to condemn him like that, to look at him in
that way? It troubled and nagged at him, her contempt. It marred his swaggering progress through
downtown Saigon; it sapped his confidence and aloof
reserve as he pushed his way through the pimps and
beggars; it made his hurried sex with the other prosti-
tutes more grimy and unsatisfactory. Nobody, he declared, knew more about hate than he did; surely no
one had hated so intensely; but this chick . . . He was
prepared, even willing, to accept the scorn and spite of
the peasant for the armed invader, but the look in that
girl's eyes had seemed to mark him out personally for
her wrath.

So on the last afternoon of his last day, Lydecker sat
in the bar and studied her, his mind a jostling crowd of
vague tensions, obscure guilts and unresolved lusts. He
was due to pick up a helicopter in a few hours that would
ferry him back to the fleet on the Yankee Station. He
felt disturbed, hung over, sullen. Saigon had proved no
release, no real solace. He felt immensely fatigued at
the thought of returning to the catapult maintenance
crew.

The bar was quiet in the afternoon's torpor. The
whores lounged in groups around the wall; some ARVN
soldiers played cards in a corner. Lydecker stared at the
girl as she swept the floor. Her hair was tied up with a
scrap of pink ribbon; her chemise shone crisply white.

Once her gaze passed over him as he sat there but there was no flicker of recognition, no revulsion or even acknowledgment in her motionless face.

As the time drew nearer for his departure, Lydecker was seized with a restless panic at the thought of leaving with so much uncertain and unfinished. He felt the sweat pool against his body, and his uniform chafed. He drank beer after beer in an attempt to keep cool.

With an hour to go, he beckoned one of the whores over. She had become something of a favorite with him and she now slid easily onto his knee. Her smile was wide and at once she started to whisper endearments and run her sharp fingers through his hair. Lydecker shrugged her hands away. For some reason the artifice and dishonesty repulsed him. He pointed to the thin girl.

"What about her?" he demanded hoarsely. "How much?"

The whore looked archly offended, hurt. "She no good. Not for G.I. She number ten, Johnny, she quick-time girl. No ficky-fick." She made a contemptuous jerking with her hand.

With a sudden movement Lydecker brutally tipped her from his lap and strode across the room toward the girl. He dropped a handful of notes on the bar in front of the startled *patron* and, seizing the girl's hand, dragged her out to the cabins at the back.

He pushed her into the first room. Solid slabs of sunlight beaming through the shutters sectioned the floor and the grubby coverlet on the bed. It was stiflingly hot. With a finger Lydecker sluiced perspiration from his forehead and upper lip. He stuffed the rest of his notes into the girl's unresponsive hand.

"Okay," he croaked. "Christ damn you. Let's really give you something to get riled over. Take 'em off." He pulled off his own clothes in a hasty flurry of movement, leaving only his shorts. The rough concrete of the floor cooled the soles of his feet. Sweat dampened the sparse black hairs on his pale chest. There was the distant sound of a Honda revving.

Very slowly the girl pocketed the money and tugged her hair free from the ribbon. She slipped the sandals from her feet and gently unwound the cloth from around her waist. The swish of material sent dust motes spiraling among the sun bars.

Without removing her chemise she went and lay on the bed. Lydecker stood, his chest heaving, his erection straining against his cotton undershorts.

"I said take it *all* off." He spoke quietly, a tremble in his voice.

The girl did nothing, her hands clenched by her slim brown thighs.

"All of it, baby. That means the fuckin' shirt." Lydecker awkwardly slipped down his shorts and moved over to stand by the bed. The girl didn't look at him.

"I'm waiting," Lydecker said harshly.

In response the girl raised the hem of her chemise to her waist and spread her legs. Lydecker gulped. A blob of sweat fell from the tip of his nose.

Suddenly he grabbed the girl's hand and jerked her roughly to her feet.

"Take it off!" he shouted. "I fuckin' *paid* you."

"No," the girl said evenly. "No good."

Lydecker seized her and crushed his mouth on hers, clashing their teeth together. Then Lydecker drew back. He had seen her eyes. On fire with disgust. Ashamed and angry, he wrenched at the chemise. It tore slightly at the shoulder. At the sound of the ripping cotton the girl's eyes registered alarm.

"No, Johnny," she said as though only half-remembering the unfamiliar whore's argot. "No good." She made vague passing movements with her hands in front of her face and soft explosion noises in the back of her throat. "Number ten. No lie G.I. Not good for you, Johnny."

What the fuck was she talking about? Lydecker wondered in desperation, as her thin hands still swooped to and fro.

"Strip, damn you. Off. All of it," he gasped.

She saw she could do nothing more. His purple swollen sex stood out from his belly like a clenched fist salute, an absurd symbol of his domination. Crossing her arms in front of her, she swiftly pulled off the chemise.

Lydecker looked at the firm, pubescent girl's body. "That's more like it, baby," he said, trying to sound kind. "I ain't gonna hurt you." His gaze cautiously returned once again to her eyes, hoping to find some more amicable response. "What's all the trouble been about, eh? C'mon, honey." But then he was perturbed to see a look of almost contemptuous triumph cross her face. She turned abruptly to reveal her back. And as she turned, Lydecker's beer-numbed mind grasped feebly at the reasons for her evasiveness. "It's all right, baby," he said reflexively, but it was too late by then.

When he saw her back, Lydecker's brain screamed in silent horror. His hands rose involuntarily to his mouth. The girl looked at him over her shoulder.

"Nay-pom," she said quietly in explanation. "Nay-pom, G.I."

Lydecker wrenched his bulging eyes away. Her back was a broad stripe, a swath of purpled shiny skin where static waves of silvery scar tissue and blistered burn weals tossed in a horrifying flesh-sea.

Lydecker emptied his stomach into his cupped hands, and his vomit splashed over his naked body.

On the Sea King taking him back to the *Chester B.*,
Lydecker sat slumped in white-faced, silent depression.
The throb of the rotor's beat sounded remorselessly in
his head. He considered his hatred and the girl's. Now
he knew why he had been so fascinated by her. They
were the same. Siblings. He looked into her eyes to find
himself staring back. They were both burning up inside with their hate and it was wrong. Their hate had
no consequences outside of themselves. It made them
sick, ate them up. It accrued only inside of them, like a
miser's hoard, poisoning everything. Their bodies
couldn't nourish such a parasite for long. Lydecker saw
that. He didn't want to end up like that girl. Infernal
decades of grief and agony beamed out from those eyes.
Perhaps what he needed was to cast it out into the world
and let it flourish there. Like Pfitz did.

As the Sea King approached the carrier, a great steel
playing field plowing through the choppy waters of the
South China Sea, Lydecker was aware of a palpable
change going through his body. He felt his breathing
become shallower and perspiration break out on his
forehead. It seemed as if his chest were hollow and filled
with throbbing, pulsating air.

Lydecker reported sick on landing and was found to
be running a high temperature. The shipboard medics
shot him full of penicillin and told him not to report
for duty for two days. During that time Lydecker
uneasily roved the corridors of the ship, a thinner and
more consumptive figure than before, his mind obsessed with the violent images of his shore leave; of his
casual unsatisfactory sex, fragments of obscene anecdotes he had heard, murmured accounts of battle-zone
atrocities, and above them all, endlessly repeating itself
like a video film loop, the vision of the young girl's
ghastly pirouette to expose her ravaged back.

Even Lydecker's normally uninterested crew-mates commented on his yellowish pallor, the sheen of sweat forever on his forehead and upper lip, his staring red-rimmed eyes. They jokingly accused him of contracting some recondite strain of venereal disease and roared with laughter when he tried haltingly to tell them about the whore and her loathsome scars.

Gradually the nomadic circuit of Lydecker's thoughts began to focus once again on Pfitz and his Crusader. Covertly, he haunted the below-deck hangar, distantly supervised the fueling and rearming of the plane, observed Pascual and Huq trundle the fat napalm canisters from the magazine elevators. He even took to following Pfitz discreetly whenever he moved from the officers' quarters, studying the man's corridor-filling bulk, the contours of his large skull revealed by his razored crew-cut, the pink fleshiness of his neck above the stiff collar of his flying suit. The glimmerings of an idea began to form in Lydecker's mind. He started to plot his revenge.

His nervous debility persisted, his temperature was regularly above normal and he collected sickness chits without problem.

Then one afternoon he was lounging in a hatchway a few feet from the Crusader's arming bay. Pfitz was talking to Lee Otis as the mechanic checked a faulty shackle on a napalm canister. Lydecker strained to catch his words.

". . . Yeah, there just ain't nothing to beat this jelly, man. It's gonna win us the woah. Shit, I can remember the original stuff. It wasn't so hot. If the dinks were quick enough they could scrape it off. So the scientists come up with a good idea. They started adding polystyrene—yeah, polystyrene. Hell, man, now it sticks better 'n shit to a blanket." He chortled. Lee Otis's eyes were glazed with boredom but Pfitz carried on, unaware in his enthusiasm. "Trouble was, if the dinks were fast enough and jumped underwater, it stopped burning. So some wise guy adds white phosphorus to the mix, and—get this, boy—now it can burn *underwater*." He reached down and patted the nose cone of the canister. "That thing on okay, now?"

Crouched in his hatchway, Lydecker waited and watched until Pfitz hauled his bulky body into the narrow cockpit of the Crusader. He tasted acid bile in his throat, his fretting hands picked unconsciously at his olive green jacket and a slight shivering ran through his wasted body. It was clear now. Beyond doubt. He couldn't understand why he had waited so long. Pfitz was the guilty one. For that girl's sake, Pfitz had to suffer too.

It didn't take Lydecker long to work out the technicalities of his revenge. The next day he was back on the catapult crew, silent and withdrawn, waiting for his time. In the evenings, with a rubber-based glue bought from the PX, and with sand from the fire buckets, and spare bolts and shards of metal from the machine rooms, he packed the beer can Pfitz had thrown at him with this glutinous hard-setting amalgam until it weighed heavy in his hand, a bright solid cylinder. To his fixated mind it had seemed only right that the beer can should be the agent of Pfitz's destruction. There was a kind of macabre symmetry in the way events were turning out that he found deeply satisfying.

Patiently, Lydecker studied the mission rotas and the catapult launch schedules, waiting for the day when Pfitz was to be first in line.

It was a bright, windy afternoon that day on the Yankee Station. The mission was close support on some hostile ville on the Cambodian border. Pfitz was in a good mood. He had just heard that he was getting a new Phantom the day after tomorrow. First in the flight, he was towed into position on the catapult and waited with his canopy up for the *Chester B.* to get up steam and turn into the wind. He saw the rescue helicopters take off and assume their positions a hundred yards out from the sides of the carrier. Pfitz looked at the catapult crew hunched against the rush of wind with their thick goggles and macrocephalic helmets. He saw the thin figure of that shithead Lydecker staring up at him, the wire launch bridle dangling from his hand. Little bastard. He began to feel uncomfortable at the insistent way Lydecker was looking at him. He seemed to remember seeing too much of the little creep around lately. He'd have to kick his butt in when he got back, get the S.O.B. to keep his distance. He hauled down his canopy as he heard the crackle of instructions in his earphones preparing him for takeoff and the Rose Train's thirty-fifth mission. As he ran through the final cockpit checks he noticed the hunched, beetling figure of Lydecker scuttling up to the nose wheel to secure the catapult bridle. As he moved out of his vision, Pfitz reflected that he'd never really taught the little shit a proper lesson; he should have had him transferred right away.

Lydecker paused for a moment at the nose of the Crusader, out of Pfitz's line of sight, buffeted by the rush of wind. For an instant he rested his gloved hand on the side of the plane and felt it shuddering from the power of its engine. His ear-muffles dampened all noise to a muted seashell roar. Then he crouched down and fitted both ends of the cables to the shackles on the nose wheel, looping the middle over the protruding shark's fin of the towing block. He knelt at the front of the plane for a second as if in supplication. And then, making sure his body obscured the view of the catapult officer, he swiftly withdrew the heavy beer can from his jacket and slotted it neatly into the recessed track, like a stubby bolt in a crossbow, just in front of the towing block.

Pfitz should have an unimpeded, normal takeoff until the towing block reached the end of the catapult track. Then there would be a slight but vital check to the momentum imparted by the tons of steam pressure driving the block, as it obliterated the solid can, jamming its clear run to the end of the track. It would be a slight, almost unnoticeable impediment but, Lydecker had calculated, a crucial one.

Lydecker ran back to his station and waved okay to the catapult officer, who barely acknowledged Lydecker's signal. It was just one launch among hundreds he had supervised, another routine mission. Nothing would happen. You were remote on the Yankee Station, the battles were elsewhere, over the horizon. Nobody attacked you and you never saw the people you atomized, shattered and burned.

Lydecker saw Pfitz lock into full afterburn. The catapult officer swept his arm forward. The seaman across the deck punched the black rubber button on the console and the catapult's release sent the Crusader blasting down the track.

Only Lydecker observed the tiny explosion as the towing block ploughed through the can, grinding it into the end of the track. A minute, inconsequential impact. But the effect on Pfitz's Crusader was dramatic. Instead of being thrown up at an angle into the skies, the plane was flung down a shallow slope into the sea some two hundred yards in front and to the left of the carrier. It was over in a couple of seconds. With a huge gout of spray, the Crusader was flipped into the sea, salt water flooding into the gaping intake, the screaming jets plunging the fully loaded aircraft deep under the surface.

There were shouts of alarm from the deck, but everything happened too quickly. Within moments they passed the spot where Pfitz had gone down; bubbling crazy water, a slick of oil, and men claimed to see the pale shape of the Crusader slipping ever deeper beneath the green surface of the sea.

Pfitz never came up and there was no further trace of the plane. The end of the catapult was found to be slightly warped and scarred, and the accident was put down to yet another malfunction. The day's mission was aborted while the mechanism was taken apart.

Lydecker stood on the edge of the deck and looked out to where the rescue helicopters futilely hovered above the oil slick. Groups of men stood about and talked of the accident. Lydecker's heart was racing and his eyes were bright. Pfitz and his napalm somewhere at the bottom of the South China Sea. He felt good. No, he felt magnificent. He wanted to bite the stars.

Histoire Vache

"So you are still a virgin," Pierre-Etienne said trium-
phantly, stubbing out his cigarette.

It had to come out, Eric thought. They had been
talking earnestly about sex all afternoon. Under cross-
examination Eric had mentioned an older girl-cousin
called Jean and suggestively introduced the notion of a
seaside holiday and a sand dune picnic *à deux*. He had
tried to keep the details vague, but conversations of this
sort remorselessly turned towards the specific and Pierre-
Etienne and Momo (Maurice) had been unsparing in
their search for the truth. They had really pinned him
down this time. Yes or no, they demanded; did you or
didn't you?

"I don't believe it," Momo said. "You never?"

Eric shook his head, trying to smile away his blush.
They were sitting at a café in the main square of Villers-
Bocage. It was market day and the place was full of
livestock and people. Momentarily Eric's attention was
distracted by the sight of a red-faced farmer in the typical knee-length Normandy blouson, energetically tugging on the tail of a cow as if he were trying to wrench
it out by the roots. Eric winced.

He looked back at his two companions. Pierre-Etienne
was the same age as he; last Easter he'd spent two weeks
in England at Eric's home. Momo was Pierre-Etienne's

brother, a little older—nearly seventeen—plump and trying to grow a moustache. Eric didn't like him that much; his air of amused tolerance towards the two younger boys was extremely irritating. Momo had a girl-friend of sorts, Eric knew, but he'd never seen Pierre-Etienne with one.

Eric sipped his *Diabolo-menthe*. He adored the chill green drink, clear and clinking with ice cubes. It was the best thing about France, he decided. He'd never learn the language, he was sure, and as far as he was concerned it wasn't worth the last two weeks of his summer holiday. Pierre-Etienne's father was the director of the Villers-Bocage abattoir, and as a result of his job the family ate meat for every meal; every sort and cut imaginable: pork, veal, beef, kidneys, heart, brains, revolting spongy tripe, lamb, oxtails, trotters, fatty purple sausages, all of it pink and undercooked and oozing with blood. Eric was returning directly to school in three days and he sometimes found himself longing for shepherd's pie or a thick Bisto stew.

"But surely you're one—a virgin—too?" he said to Pierre-Etienne in half-hearted counter-attack.

"Of course not." Pierre-Etienne looked offended.

"But you don't have a girl-friend," Eric said. "How could you?"

"No," Momo said, "he don't have a girl-friend, but he has Marguerite."

"And who's she?"

Marguerite Grosjean shouted goodbye to her mother and eased her bulk into her tiny 2-CV. As usual her mother didn't reply. Marguerite lit her fifth Gauloise of the day. She sat for a moment in her car. It was only half past five and Villers-Bocage was just ten minutes away through early morning mist. She puffed on her

cigarette and scratched her thigh. Her mother leaned
out of the upstairs window and shouted at her. It was
just a noise. Her mother ran out to the car screaming
abuse. Marguerite flipped down the window. Arcs of
spittle from her mother's mouth spattered on the glass.
Marguerite let it go on a few seconds. It was like this
every morning. Then she started the engine and drove
off, leaving the small dishevelled figure, still shaking with
rage, alone in the yard.

She arrived at the abattoir a little early so she went
to the nearby bar and ordered a *café-calva*. The waiter
brought her the drink. He was new to the café. He
smiled and said good morning but Marguerite appeared not to notice him. He found this somewhat unusual, as he had taken her against the wall at the back
of the café only three nights ago when she came off
night shift. He said good morning again but she didn't
reply. He shrugged his shoulders and walked off, but
he kept the tab. It wasn't much but it was something.
One of the butchers who worked in the abattoir had told
him about Marguerite and all the butchers, farm-hands,
meat packers and lorry drivers. You just need to ask,
the man had said, that's all, a simple request, and he
had tapped his temple with a forefinger. The waiter had
met her on her way back from the toilet. The butcher
had been right.

He thought of asking her again, just now, to see if it
was really true, but the clear morning light was unkind
to the fat woman so he went on wiping the tables.

Eric, Pierre-Etienne and Momo stood at the back of the
abattoir looking over a wall at the stream of departing
workers from the morning shift.

"Which one is she?" Eric asked.

"That one there, the big one, going in the car."

Eric saw lots of cars and quite a few large women.

"Which car?" he asked.

"That one," Momo said, pointing to an old 2-CV being driven away. Eric couldn't really see the driver, just a white face and black hair.

He felt a thump of excited pressure in his chest. "What do I have to do?" he asked.

"You just go and tell her what you want," Pierre-Etienne said.

"Is that *all*? Just ask?"

"Yes, it's all."

"But why does she do it? Do . . . do I have to pay her or anything?"

The two French boys laughed delightedly. "No, no," Momo said. "She do it for nothing. She likes it."

"Oh," said Eric knowledgeably, "a nympho. But are you sure? You're not lying? She does it just like that?"

"Everybody is going to Marguerite," Momo said with emphasis. "*We* have gone."

"Bloody hell. Did *you*?" Eric asked Pierre-Etienne.

"Of course," he replied. "I have been three times. It is easy."

"God," said Eric quietly. The ease of the whole venture astonished him. It really was going to happen. "But I still don't understand *why*. What for? Why does she do it?"

Marguerite parked her car at the back of the abattoir near the packed cattle pens full of grunting and shifting beasts. As she walked into the room where she worked the familiar pungent ammoniacal smell of guts and excrement tickled her nostrils. She took her plastic overall off the peg and buttoned it tightly across her massive chest. She stepped into her gumboots and pulled the white cap over her wiry black hair, just beginning to be streaked with grey.

She heard the men arrive, the jokes and the early

morning banter. A few stepped in for a moment and said hello. She stood looking at the huge stainless-steel basins. She leant back against the mangle. She wasn't thinking about anything, just waiting for Marcel to wheel in the first tub of shivering, gelid, brown and purple guts.

Then she heard the familiar sound of the slaughter begin. The compressed-air *phut* of the humane killer as the retractable six-inch spike was driven into the animal's skull. The clang as the side of the pen fell away to let the beast tumble down the concrete incline, the rattle of its hooves on the cement. Then there was the whirr of the hoist as the carcass was lifted up by a rear leg and almost simultaneously the splash as the blood poured from twin slits made in the throat. It took barely a minute for the skin to be removed before the buzzing circular saw carved down the length of the suspended body, opening it wide. The first today was a cow; she recognised the second splash—this time of milk—as the udder was halved by the whining blade. Then there was the slithering, slopping waterfall as the insides fell out. The moan of the overhead rails—as the carcass was swung down the line to the butchers and the cavernous refrigerating plant—was punctuated by the thumps and splashings of the second animal being killed.

Eight cows later, Marcel wheeled in the first of the buckets. He was simple and had a harelip. He never spoke much. He turned on the hoses and water sprays and plunged his bare hands into the gelatinous mass of entrails and heaved great piles into the brimming sinks. There were arm-length rubber gloves for this purpose but Marcel maintained that they only made his job harder.

Marguerite stood above the overflowing steaming basins and quickly sorted the larger pieces of offal from the long strings of intestines. She flung the stomachs onto a recessed tray which Marcel later took through to the tripe room. Her overalls were soon covered by a green slime of blood and feculence. She took a bucket of the washed viscera over to the mangle and forced an end of gut between the rollers. She grunted slightly as she turned the handle to run them through. Green and purple efflux plopped and spouted from the other end, splashing onto her boots and the floor, where it was hosed into the drains by Marcel.

Pale emptied ropes of intestine were collected in a zinc bucket on the other side of the mangle. Marguerite gave them a final wash-through with a high-pressure hose to remove all remaining particles before Marcel took them to be prepared for tripe. She worked on this way until lunchtime, pausing occasionally to smoke a cigarette or take a drink from a bottle of Calvados she kept on a window ledge.

That night Eric lay in bed thinking about the next day. It was all arranged for lunchtime. Apparently Marguerite always ate lunch in her car. Momo was going to write a note for him to give to her. That was all he had to do.

Eric wondered what it would be like. What it would feel like. He wondered what Morton and Haines would say when he told them back at school. Was it going to be any different from when he did it himself? He slipped his hand into his pyjama trousers and touched himself, ran his fingers over his neat bush of pubic hair. He couldn't imagine it at all. It seemed so easy. What if something went wrong?

The three boys were waiting at the back of the abattoir by eleven o'clock. Eric kept clearing his throat, and his palms were wet with perspiration even though it was a cool morning. Momo had written out the brief note; he was being especially nice that day.

"What is it I have to say?" Eric asked for the tenth time.

"Just say, 'Vous êtes Madame Marguerite?' and give her the note."

"Vous êtes Madame Marguerite?"

"Good," Momo said. "Très bien," and handed him the piece of paper. Eric unfolded it. Momo had printed in block letters "JE VOUDRAIS TE SAUTER GROSSE TRUIE."

"What does it mean?" Eric asked Pierre-Etienne.

"It means: 'I want to make love with you, you lovely woman.' "

Eric frowned. "Are you sure? I always thought *sauter* meant to jump."

"Oh, it's an expression you can use," Pierre-Etienne said quickly, glancing at Momo, who added, "It's a more agreeable way to say it."

"Ah. I see. Okay."

When Marguerite appeared, Eric was surprised at how big she was. When she climbed into her car it tossed on its springs like a boat in a storm. At once a blind funk seized him and he felt convinced that he wouldn't be able to go through with it. But Momo and Pierre-Etienne were urging him on relentlessly, as if they were aware of the weight of self-doubt building up in his mind. The consequences of backing out at this stage were too severe to be contemplated; the immense agonies of shame and abuse that would have to be endured. It was too late for second thoughts now. In any case he felt strangely cushioned from events and embarrassment by the barrier of language; it was like watching yourself on a home movie. Besides, if she swore at him or called the police he just wouldn't understand, and anyway, he was going home tomorrow.

However, as he crunched across the gravel of the car-park he felt very lonely and exposed. He looked back at Pierre-Etienne and Momo, who eagerly waved him on. They had made it sound like the most natural thing in the world, something any youth in Villers-Bocage did as a matter of course—an easy initiation. There had been disparaging remarks about the effeminate, gelded sissies who balked at the opportunity. *"Ils sont vraiment les gonzesses, les tantouzes."* Eric asked what they were. *"Les pédés, homosexuels,"* plump Momo said, his voice hoarse with disdain. Now as he walked across the car-park he felt the gaze of the two boys at his back like a goad.

Marguerite sat in the passenger seat of her small car, which listed heavily. She had finished her sandwich. Eric looked at her forearm, which rested on the sill. It was very white, white as a fridge, and large and soft. There was a dark shadow of hairs running down it. Her fingernails were rimmed with what looked like brown ink.

Eric cleared his throat. *"Êtes-vous Madame Marguerite?"* he asked, holding out the note.

"Êtes-vous Madame Marguerite?"

Marguerite looked round. The boy was standing against the light and at first she couldn't really see him. She took the note he was holding but he didn't go away. She opened it up and read the message. She felt her face grow hot with anger and her mouth tightened. To her surprise the boy remained standing; she had expected to see him scampering off, laughing delightedly at his filthy joke. But he was not even smiling; he seemed a little nervous.

Marguerite opened the door of the car and got out. She folded her arms across her bosom and glared at the

boy. He was tall and slender with straight blond hair
that fell across his forehead. His face was awkward and
uneven with adolescence, as if he'd borrowed some features from a larger person. He had small pink spots at
the corners of his mouth and on his chin.

"*Ah, bon,*" she said, her anger making her voice tremble. "*Tu veux m'sauter.*"

"Um . . . ah, *pardon?*" the boy said.

She heard his accent. Her anger began to fade. It
never lasted long anyway. The joke was on him. "*Anglais?*" she asked.

He nodded. Marguerite looked round for his friends,
the ones who had played the joke, but she couldn't see
anyone. She flourished the note.

"*C'est ordurier ça.*" But he didn't understand her. His
quick smile was nervous and uncertain and she suddenly felt sorry for him. She breathed out slowly and
looked at him again. The anger had barely rippled the
placid lake of her total indifference. She seldom let her
mind contribute anything to the flow of experience. It
had only brought her anguish and difficulty. So now she
passively received the sensations it threw at her. She had
no doubts and she had no complaints.

"Okay," she said and beckoned him to follow. She led
him out of the car-park and round a corner to a cluster
of outbuildings, garages and store-rooms. She opened
a wooden door at the back of a garage and showed him
in. On the wall a shelf of sunlight from a high window
illuminated some old packing-cases and cardboard boxes.
In the corner was a bed of sorts: a mattress and a blanket. There were a grimy sink and a table and a chair.
Some newspapers and magazines lay on the table. The
room was used by the security guards; somewhere to
go if the rain was heavy, a place for an undisturbed
smoke and a chat, somewhere to take Marguerite.

She came up behind the boy, who was looking round him uncomfortably. She touched his hair; it was very clean and shiny. He was surprised and glanced round quickly, automatically raising a hand to the back of his head. Marguerite smiled at him, enjoying his youth and his reticence.

"*Vas y,*" she said, pointing to the mattress. The boy started to unbutton his shirt and slipped it off his shoulders. He kicked off his shoes. Marguerite was surprised; no man had ever bothered to undress for her before—at the most, trousers were lowered to the knees—and she removed only what was essential.

The boy stood there in his underpants, uneasy in the intensity of her gaze. With a start she realised he was waiting for her to undress. She looked at his hairless body, the slim legs, the shadows of his ribs, the lean jut of his pelvis, and he seemed to her almost painfully beautiful. As she fumbled with the buttons on her dress she felt a strange thick sensation in her throat, and for a brief moment the utter grief of her life cut like a razor and her eyes spangled with tears.

Eric lay still in Marguerite's arms. She was holding him tight, running her hands up and down his body, muttering soft phrases that he couldn't understand. Eric was aware of an unfamiliar tiredness, and now that it was all over he longed to be away from this small room and this large white woman with her curious smell. At the beginning he had been numbed and filled with nervousness when she had taken off her clothes and lain down beside him on the mattress. What struck him was not the heavy flat breasts with their stark brown nipples, the bushy armpits or the overhanging belly, but the shocking nude whiteness of the woman. She was so white she was almost grey, as he remembered his arm had once been when it was removed from a plaster cast.

The brief, unsatisfactory coupling was completed within seconds, or so it seemed to Eric, who now ran through his past sensations like a clerk at a filing cabinet, seeking for something that was memorable, that retained traces of excitement. She had kissed his face and rolled him on top of her, manipulating and pushing him around like a worker he'd once seen operating a die stamper. But now it was over, she just seemed to want to hold him and Eric didn't know what to do. And there was the smell. At first he thought it came from the mattress but then he realised it rose from her skin, a thin acidic smell, almost organic and living.

Eric was confused about his role; it had not been like the books he'd read or the stories he'd heard. He had been passive, merely fulfilling a function. He hadn't felt anything. Once, when waiting for the school train, Haines had pointed to a group of women in black overalls who were carrying long brushes and heading up the platform towards the sidings. The women who cleaned the carriages, Haines said, were notorious. They'd do it for ten bob, anywhere, with anyone.

Tentatively Eric brought his hand up from the mattress and touched Marguerite's breast. The nipple was coarse and thick like a small brown raspberry. His palm cautiously inched up the slack bulge of her breast. He gently touched the nipple and let his fingers trickle over it. As he touched it she said something and hugged him close to her with a strength he found surprising, so that he felt in a moment of panic that the viscid-white flesh might envelop him, lapping round his body like mud. She reached down for him, her other hand pressing his face into her neck, and he could smell her; he could feel it filling his lungs like water.

With a wriggle he broke free and sat up. He pointed

to his watch. "I have to go," he said, and quickly pulled on his clothes. Marguerite, alone on the mattress and suddenly aware of her nakedness, covered herself with her dress.

Eric crouched in the corner tying up his shoelaces, his face hot with embarrassment, unable to say a word, the silence heavy in the air like a threat. From the corner of his eye he saw her leg, the purple-veined thigh with its furze of dark hairs, and he felt his top lip twitch with distaste. He went over to her, carefully avoiding her gaze and breathing through his mouth.

Marguerite was very quiet. Eric reached into his pocket and withdrew two ten-franc notes. "Here." He held them out. "Merci," he added, feeling foolish. But she just curled his fingers back round them and pushed his hand away. For a moment his hand with the notes seemed to hover disconnectedly between them. Suddenly Eric wished she had taken the money. It would have been better.

"Well, goodbye," he said. "*Au revoir.*"

Outside, the air felt washed and fragrant. Eric took deep breaths and tried to lift the mood he sensed was descending on him as inevitably as night. . . .

The afternoon sun beat down on him. It was that curious pause in the year: high summer slipping into autumn. Things started to decay then: wars began; dogs went mad. The green of the trees and the grass looked tired, old and tramped-on.

"How was it?" Pierre-Etienne asked when Eric caught up with them.

"Fantastic," Eric lied automatically.

"You were a long time," Momo said.

"Was I? Oh, well, you know how it is."

"Did you . . . really?" Pierre-Etienne asked.
Eric looked at him curiously. "Yes. It went just like
you said." He shivered. "She's big. Huge . . . you know."
He weighed two mammoth breasts in front of him.
Pierre-Etienne and Momo looked on with ill-con-
cealed amazement. Eric said, *"Elle pue,"* and they both
laughed uneasily. He touched his back pocket and heard
the crinkle of notes. He turned and walked away from
the abattoir back towards the market-place. Pierre-
Etienne and Momo followed behind, deep in conversation.

"Come on," Eric shouted, "I'll buy you a *Diabolo-
menthe.*"

Marcel looked up in surprise when Marguerite said
goodbye. Normally they parted without a word. She
went to the café and ordered a drink. The late afternoon sun cast long shadows across the street; a slight
breeze shifted a scrap of paper on the pavement; am-
ber light flashed momentarily from a chrome bumper.
Some of the butchers from the day shift came into the
café but she paid them no attention. She was thinking
about clean shiny hair, smoothness, a touch.

She called for another *calva.* She would go home late
tonight, maybe see a film or just sit on here in the café
for a while. It was a pleasant evening. There was something solid and achieved about the depth of the shadows, it seemed to her; the kindness of the yellowy sun
patches on the table tops pleased her obscurely. She took
the last sip of *calva.* The English boy had been gentle
and she had made him happy.

The waiter brought her new drink over. As he put it
down he whispered his request in her ear. She looked
round. The man leant confidentially over the table. She

saw his oily hair, his silver tooth, his shiny watch.
"Well?" he asked, smiling, his eyebrows raised.

"No," said Marguerite abruptly, before she had really
even thought about it. "No. Tomorrow perhaps, we'll
see. But not today. Not today."

My Girl
in Skintight Jeans

I would like to make one thing clear before I tell my story. I don't want you to think that because I have never married that there is any kind of . . . of a problem between me and the female sex. I could in fact have married any number of girls had I so chosen—but I didn't choose to, so there it is. It was a question of my health, you see. I do not have a strong constitution and largely for that reason I decided, once my dear mother had died, to remain a bachelor.

My mother left me a small legacy along with the house. I live quietly and economically there. I have several projects with which I am currently occupied and they take up a fair amount of my time. I am a great reader, too, and one of the luxuries of not having to work for a living is that I can indulge to the full my passion for reading. Lately, however, I have grown rather tired of books and for the last year or so have read only magazines. I have subscriptions to thirty-eight and buy many others on a casual, sporadic basis. I read all kinds except the political ones; I like the bright, happy illustrations and I have been progressively coming around to the opinion that magazines are, indeed, more imaginative than many novels. The world of the glossy magazine holds more allure for me than the grimy realistic tragedies that pass for literature these days. Every winter I leave the house, board it up and switch off the water and electricity. I spend the winter months in a small resort town a few miles up the coast from San Luis Obispo in northern California. I get all my magazine subscriptions forwarded there. It's a quiet life, but cheap and necessary for my health. Over the years I've got to know most of the inhabitants, but they're not very sociable folk and I find that few of them have much to say for themselves.

This last winter had been a bad one for me. My budget, due to the failure of one of my projects, was lower than ever and my life-style was correspondingly reduced. I had been chronically depressed through most of January and February and if it hadn't been for the regular arrival of my magazines with their laughing happy people in their primary-colored world, I'm sure I would have done something drastic. However, as spring approached, my spirits rallied and I began to feel a little better.

Then she arrived—a modern *primavera*—and the sleepy resort town seemed to respond to her exciting presence. I began to think of her possessively as "my girl." She was definitely my kind of girl. My girl in skintight jeans, I called her. It was merely a fancy of mine; I never actually plucked up the courage to introduce myself. I saw her regularly every day from my room and soon grew to feel that somehow I had come to know her, got to grips with what I believe is a rare, remarkable personality.

She's beautiful too. Shaggy, clean blond hair, a short, crisp white T-shirt leaving a gap of navel-dimpled caramel belly between its hem and her dark, tight navy jeans. Those long-legged, tapered blue jeans.

It makes me feel good to think of her as my girl. For some reason she always wears the same outfit every day—but it's always fresh and well laundered. She's the most truly at-ease person I've ever come across: there's an astonishing serenity that beams out of her eyes. I have noticed, too, that she never wears a brassiere, and the thin material of her T-shirt is molded closely to her breasts.

My room is small but I keep it tidy. There's an electric ring and a sink in the corner but I don't do much cooking because I hate the smell it leaves. My room is on the top floor of an old building on the seafront. It has two windows and from one of them I can get a good view of the ocean and the coast. In this town only two cafés stay open through the winter season and I divide my meals more or less equally between them; I don't wish to seem particular and have no desire to give offense. In fact I prefer the Del Mar, but I don't want to alienate old Luke who runs Luke 'n' Loretta's. He's nearly blind, but we talk a lot and I kind of like the old guy. I'm unwilling to tell him but, as his sight's got worse, so has his place. Nowadays he leaves nearly everything up to his sister, Loretta. She's an overweight, red-rinsed whore who lives in a camping truck out in back. For five dollars she'll give you a quick time out there. Believe me, it isn't worth it. For some reason though, she's taken a shine to me—asked me around for a drink after closing a couple of times. But since the girl in skintight jeans arrived I've stayed away. Then Loretta cut me dead in the street yesterday so I thought I'd better go back, just to keep the peace.

There was the first spring-quickening in the air this morning as I walked to Luke's for breakfast. A watery sun warmed the sea breeze; the day was mild with a light-blue sky up above. However, any elation I felt was dissipated when I got to Luke's. There was no sign of the old man and the place was a real toilet. I sat at my usual table and waited for Loretta to come and clear it up. It was swimming with spilled coffee, the ashtray was full of butts and someone had ground out a cigar in a half-eaten plate of pancakes and syrup. Loretta wore a loose Hawaiian blouse and stretch slacks in honor of the clement weather. She sat down and chatted and offered me one of the menthol cigarettes she chain-smokes, so I guessed I must have been forgiven. Then she leaned right over in front of me while she cleared the table so I could get a good look down her front at her heavy breasts. I ordered a hot tea, no milk, with a slice of lemon.

It may have been warmer outside but Loretta wasn't taking any chances. All the windows were tight shut and their film of condensation and grease obscured any view of the beach.

I heard a car pull up. I wiped the window and peered out. It was a battered convertible and there were three guys inside. They got out and stretched, rubbing their buttocks and looking around. They were young, two whites and a Hispanic. There was a thin one with a pimp's moustachio and a thick-lipped, black-haired guy with oddly white tattooed arms. They were wearing worn-out sharpie clothes.

This is a quite little town we live in and I hoped they'd just move on through. But just then the sun came out from behind some clouds, and in the corner of my eye, I caught its flash on the girl's white T-shirt. It was the first time I'd seen her that day and I wiped the window some more to get a better look. But they saw her, too, and they glanced at one another and laughed in that

shifty, teeth-baring way men in a group have. One of
them bent his arm and did something with his fingers
while the thick-lipped guy cupped his hands over his
crotch and groaned. They all laughed again.

I felt my face flush and a pulse beat at my temples.
When I put my cup down in its saucer there was a rattle of china. They disgust me, this kind of filth. City scum
degenerates, just drifting up the coast in a hot car looking for cheap kicks.

I spent the rest of the day in my room reading my
magazines. Later I tried to sleep but I had developed a
bad headache. In the afternoon I had a long shower.
That made me feel a little better.

At dusk I went to a small supermarket that I sometimes buy provisions at when I don't feel like going out
to eat. I was reaching for a can of clam chowder when
I saw the girl through the window. I was a little surprised. Usually I never managed to see her this late and
I always wondered where she went. But tonight it was
obvious. Her eyes were gazing out to sea; her easy stride
would carry her determinedly down to the beach.

The clam chowder tasted like earth. I couldn't clear my
mouth of it, so I drank a glass or two of rye. I opened
the window that gives me a sea view and sat on the sill
looking out at the darkening waters. Quite a way along
the beach I could see the glimmer of a campfire burning and I knew at once that was where the girl would
be—out there alone. Maybe she had cooked something
and was enjoying the peace and absolute solitude. Then
I could imagine her stripping off her clothes, her tan
body with white bikini patches maybe, paler in the
gloom, the breeze tensing her nut-brown nipples, the
cool of the water as the waves broke against her golden
thighs. . . .

But then I was distracted by the noise of raucous laughter in the street below. The three youths, half bombed, spilling out of the liquor store clutching six-packs and a bottle of wine. With a bizarre sense of mounting premonition I watched them laughing and joshing for a while in the street. Then one of them said, "Hey, look. A fire." And with whistles and whoops they went running down the boardwalk, all heroic with beer, jumping gleefully onto the sand and heading up the beach toward my girl.

For an instant I heard my heart booming in my skull and my eyeballs seemed to bulge rhythmically to its beat. With a forefinger I wiped beads of perspiration from my upper lip. *Bastards!* SCUM TRASH BASTARDS! I saw stubby stained fingers fondling corn-yellow hair, spectral tattooed arms circling her slim brown body, probing tongue between thick dabbing lips, young beards on soft skin. She'd come dripping from the surf, wading quietly out of the green sea, her body dim and mysterious, to find a leering drunken horror waiting around her fire.

I felt the sharp taste of vomit in my throat, for I was almost sick with a desperate fear and anxiety as I rummaged in my bureau for my gun, an old police special. I was sick with insane visions of the fabulous lusts of nightmare hooligans, terrible images of deviant sex-dreams being foully realized out there on the lonely coast.

I came up behind them through the dunes, my feet silent on the sand. The three of them sat around the fire, drunk. One of them was singing quietly to himself. Discarded beer cans lay like shell cases around a gun emplacement. There was no sign of the girl.

They heard the sound of my feet as I crossed the strip of pebbles that lay above the high-tide mark.

"Hey, man," the thick-lipped one said. "Whatcha doin'? Have a drink. Luis, give . . ."

Then he saw the gun. His jaw slackened as his beer-numbed brain tried to cope with what was happening.

"C'mon, what gives?" There was a smile of disbelief on his face. The other two began to edge away from me.

"Where is she?" I said, my voice shaking with rage and disgust. I raised my eyes, looking for signs of a shallow grave, half expecting to see her violated body cast up on the beach by the waves. "What have you filth done with her? Where is she? Where have you put her?"

He stood up shakily, an uncertain smile on his face. He looked around at his friends for support. "Who, man?" he said, shrugging his shoulders. "For chrissake, who?"

"*My girl!*" I screamed at him, maddened by his feeble attempts to protest his innocence. "My sweet girl, you bastard!"

"We ain't seen no friggin' girl, man," he shouted back, arcs of spittle flying from his lips.

The waves seemed to be crashing and breaking in my head as I leveled the gun at his denimed groin and pulled the trigger. I missed, but the bullet tore off a chunk of his thigh, which splashed a bright red in the firelight. He screamed with the pain and went down.

When the sound of the waves and the echoes of the shot had diminished, I heard the rattle of pebbles as his two friends ran off.

Thick-lips was crawling painfully down the sand toward the sea. One leg of his jeans was damp and left a trail like a slug. He was making little whimpering noises.

"I'll give you one last chance," I shouted after him. "Tell me where she is."

He said nothing.

I pocketed the gun and picked up a piece of driftwood about the size of a baseball bat. I weighed it in my hand, swishing it gently through the air to get my grip right. Then I walked down the beach to thick-lips and with five or six firm strokes battered his head into the wet sand at the surf edge. The foam went pink like a milkshake. When it was over I pushed him well out into the breakers. The tide was ebbing and it would be a couple of days before he washed up again. Then I stood on the beach and shouted out into the waves just in case she was out there. "It's okay," I shouted. "You can come out. They've gone."

But she never appeared.

When I woke up the next morning I knew instinctively she had gone forever and for a moment I felt the sadness of her passing intensely.

I went to the window and opened it and took a few deep breaths. Across the street a man was working on the billboard. Distracted, I began to admire the way he handled the huge, cumbersome folds of paper, his dexterity in spreading the sheets so accurately and with such little fuss, the precision with which he manipulated the long sopping brush. And, as the new advertisement took shape, I found I was forgetting about the girl as she disappeared, with her impossibly white T-shirt and her ludicrously skintight jeans.

I stood there at the window a while, just looking.

Yes, I thought to myself. Yes. Definitely my kind of drink. Mellow, with the real tawny glow . . .

Extracts from the Journal
of Flying Officer J

> *Duke Senior:* Stay, Jaques, stay.
> *Jaques:* To see no pastime I: what you would have
> I'll stay to know at your abandoned cave.
>   *As You Like It,* v. 4

ASCENSION

"The hills 'round here are like a young girl's breasts."
Thus Squadron Leader "Duke" Verschoyle. Verbatim.
4:30 P.M., on the lawn, loudly.

ROGATION SUNDAY

Last night ladies were invited into the mess. I went alone.
"Duke" Verschoyle took a Miss Bald, a friend of Neves'.
At supper Verschoyle, who was sufficiently intoxicated,
flipped a piece of bread at Miss Bald. She replied with
a fid of ham which caught Verschoyle smack in his grinning face. A leg of chicken was then aimed at the lady
by our Squadron Leader, but it hit me, leaving a large
grease stain on my dress jacket. I promptly asked if the

mess fund covered the cost of cleaning. I was sconced for talking shop.

Verschoyle liverish in morning.

JUNE 4

Sortie at dawn. I took the monoplane. Flew south to the Chilterns. At 7,000 feet I felt I could see every trembling blade of grass. Monoplane solid as a hill. Low-level all the way home. No sign of activity anywhere.

Talked to Stone. Says he knew Phoebe at Melton in 1923. Swears she was a brunette then.

FRIDAY, LUNCH-TIME

Verschoyle saunters up, wearing a raffish polka-dot cravat, a pipe clamped between his large teeth. Speaks without removing it. I transcribe exactly: "Msay Jks, cd yizzim psibly siyerway tklah thnewmn, nyah?" *What?* He removes his loathsome teat, a loop of saliva stretching and gleaming momentarily between stem and lip. There's a new man, it appears. Randall something or something Randall. Verschoyle wants me to run a routine security clearance.

"Very well, sir," I say.

"Call me 'Duke,' " he suggests. Fatal influence of the cinema on the service. Must convey my thoughts on the matter to Reggie.

Stone is driving me mad. His shambling, loutish walk. His constant whistling of "My Little Grey Home in the West." The way he breathes through his mouth. As far as I can see he might as well not have a nose—he never uses it

SUNDAY A.M.

French cricket by runway B. I slope off early down to The Sow & Farrow. The pub is dark and cool. Baking-hot day outside. Slice of joint on a pewter plate. Household bread and butter. A pint of turbid beer. All served up by the new barmaid, Rose. Lanky, athletic girl, strong-looking. Blonde. We chatted amiably until the rest of the squadron—in their shouting blazers and tennis shoes—romped noisily in. I left a 4*d.* tip. Strangely attractive girl.

MEMO. RANDALL'S INTERROGATION

1. Where is the offside line in a rugby scrum?
2. Is Kettner's in Church Street or Poland Street?
3. What is "squegging"? And who shouldn't do it?
4. How would you describe *Zéphire de Sole Paganini*?
5. Sing "Hey, Johnny Cope."
6. Which is the odd one out: BNC, SEH, CCC, LMH, SHC?
7. Complete this saying: "Hope springs eternal in the—."

DOMINION DAY (CANADA)

Randall arrives. Like shaking hands with a marsh. Cheerful round young face. Prematurely bald. Tufts of hair deliberately left unshaved on cheekbones. Overwhelming urge to strike him. Why do I sense the man is not to be trusted?

Verschoyle greets him like a long-lost brother. It seems they went to the same prep school. Later, Verschoyle tells me to forget about the interrogation. I point out

that it's mandatory under the terms of the draft constitution. "Duke" reluctantly has to back down.
    NB. Verschoyle's breath smelling strongly of pepper-
mint.

WEDNESDAY NIGHT

Sagging, moist evening. Sat out on the lawn till late,
writing to Reggie, telling him of Verschoyle's appalling
influence on the squadron—the constant rags, high jinks,
general refusal to take our task seriously. Started to write
about the days with Phoebe at Melton, but kept thinking of Rose. Curious.

JULY—?

Sent to Coventry by no. 3 flight for putting their drunken Welsh mechanic on a charge. Today, Verschoyle
declared the monoplane his own. I'm left with a lum-
bering old Ganymede II. It's like flying a turd. I'll have
my work cut out in a dogfight.

P.M. Map-reading class: Randall, Stone, Guy and Bede.
Stone hopeless, he'd get lost in a corridor. Randall surprisingly efficient. He seems to know the neighbour-
hood suspiciously well. Also annoyingly familiar. Asked
me if I wanted to go down to The Sow & Farrow for a
drink. I set his interrogation for Thursday, 15.00 hours.

BANK HOLIDAY MONDAY

Drove down to the coast with Rose. Unpleasant day,
scouring wind off the ice caps, grey-flannel sky. The pier
was deserted, but Rose insisted on swimming. I stamped
on the shingle beach while she changed in the dunes.

Her dark-blue woollen bathing suit flashing by as she sprinted strongly into the breakers. A glimpse of white pounding thighs, then shrieks and flailing arms. Jovial shouts of encouragement from me. She emerged, shivering, her nose endearingly red, to be enfolded in the rough towel that I held. Her front teeth slightly askew. Made my heart cartwheel with love. She said it was frightfully cold but exhilarating. Her long nipples erect for a good five minutes.

JULY 21

Boring day. Verschoyle damaged the monoplane when he flew through a mob of starlings, so he's temporarily grounded himself. He and Randall as thick as thieves. I caught them leering across the bar at Rose. Cleverly, she disguised her feelings on seeing me, knowing how I value discretion.

RANDALL'S INTERROGATION

Randall unable to complete final verse of "Hey, Johnny Cope." I report my findings to Verschoyle and recommend Randall's transfer to Movement Control. Verschoyle says he's never even heard of "Hey, Johnny Cope." He's a deplorable example to the men.

Note to Reggie: in 1914 we were fighting for our golf and our weekends.

Went to the zoological gardens and looked at the llama. Reminded me of Verschoyle. In the reptile house I saw a chameleon: repulsive bulging eyes—Randall. Peafowl—Guy. Civet cat—Miss Bald. Anteater—Stone. Gazelle—Rose. Bateleur eagle—me.

475TH DAY OF THE STRUGGLE

Three battalions attacked today, north of Cheltenham. E. went down in one of the Griffins. Ground fire. A perfect arc. Crashed horribly not two miles from Melton.

Dawn patrol along the River Lugg. The Ganymede's crude engine is so loud I fly in a perpetual swooning migraine. Struts thrumming and quivering like palsied limbs. Told a disgruntled Fielding to de-caulk cylinder heads before tomorrow's mission.

Randall returned late from a simple reconnaisance flight. He had some of us worried. Claimed a map-reading error. It was because of his skill with maps that he was put on reconnaisance in the first place. Verschoyle untypically subdued at the news from Cheltenham. Talk of moving to a new base in the Mendips.

RANDALL: Did you know that Rose was a promising young actress?
STONE: Oh, yes? What's she promised you, then?

As a result of this flash of wit. Stone was elected entertainments secretary for the mess. He plans a party before the autumn frosts set in.

63RD WEDNESDAY

On the nature of love. There are two sorts of people you love. There are people you love steadily, unreflectingly: people who you know will never hurt you. Then there are people you love fiercely: people who you know can and will hurt you.

AUGUST 1. MONDAY

Tredgold tells me that Randall was known as a trophy maniac at college. Makes some kind of perverse sense.

AUGUST 7

Luncheon with Rose at The Compleat Angler, Marlow. Menu: *Oeufs* Magenta; Mock Turtle Soup; Turbot; Curried Mutton *au riz;* Orange Jelly. Not bad for these straitened times we live in. Wines: a half bottle of Gonzalez Coronation Sherry.

SUNDAY

Tea with the Padre. Bored rigid. He talked constantly of the bout of croupous pneumonia his sister had just endured.

Suddenly realised what it was that finally put me off Phoebe. It was the way she used to pronounce the word "piano" with an Italian accent. "Would you care for a tune on the *piano?*"

AUG. 15, 17.05

Stone crash-landed on the links at Beddlesea. He was on the way back from a recce. of the new base in the Mendips. Unharmed, luckily. But the old Gadfly is seriously damaged. He trudged all the way back to the clubhouse from the 14th fairway, but they wouldn't let him use the phone because he wasn't a member.

Rose asked me today if it was true that Randall was the best pilot in the squadron. I said, don't be ridiculous.

Read Reggie's article: "Air power and the modern guerrilla."

500TH DAY OF THE STRUGGLE

It's clear that Verschoyle is growing a beard. Broadmead and Collis-Sandes deserted. They stole Stone's Humber. It's worth noting, I think, that Collis-Sandes played wing three-quarter for Blackheath.

WED. P.M.

Verschoyle's beard filmy and soft, with gaps. He looks like a bargee. The Padre seems to have taken something of a shine to yours truly. He invited me to his rooms for a drink yesterday evening. (One Madeira in a tiny clouded glass as big as my thumb, and two *petit-beurres*.) Croupous pneumonia again . . .
On the way home, stopped in my tracks by a vision of Rose. Pure and naked. Harmonious as a tree. *Rose!*
Mendip base unusable.

71ST MONDAY

Verschoyle shaves off beard. Announcement today of an historic meeting between commands at Long Hanborough.

6TH SUNDAY BEFORE ADVENT

Working late in the hangar with young Fielding (the boy is ruined with acne). Skirting through the laurels on a short cut back to the mess, I notice a torch flash three times from Randall's room.
Later, camped out on the fire escape and well bun-

dled up, I see him scurry across the moonlit lawn in dressing-gown and pyjamas with what looks like a blanket (a radio? semaphore kit? maps?), heading for the summer-house.

The next morning I lay my accusations before Verschoyle and insist on action. He places me under arrest and confines me to quarters. I get the boy Fielding to smuggle a note to Rose.

Visit from Stone. Tells me the autogiro has broken down again. News of realignments and negotiations in the cities. Drafting of the new constitution halted. Prospects of Peace. No word from Rose.

3RD DAY OF CAPTIVITY

Interviewed by Scottish psychiatrist on Verschoyle's instructions. Dr. Gilzean; strong Invernesshire accent. Patently deranged. The interview keeps being interrupted as we both pause to make copious notes. Simple ingenuous tests:

Word Association

DR. GILZEAN	ME
lighthouse —	a small aunt
cave —	tolerant grass
cigar —	the neat power station
mouth —	mild
key —	kind
lock —	speedy vans
cucumber —	public baths
midden —	the wrinkling wrists of gloves

Rorschach Blots

DR. GILZEAN

ME

"A queer nun"   "A new trug"   "A fucked hen"

Dr. Gilzean pronounces me entirely sane. Verschoyle apologizes.

FIRST DAY OF FREEDOM

Stone's party in the mess. Verschoyle suggests the gymkhana game. A twisting course of beer bottles is laid out on the lawn. The women are blindfolded and driven in a harness of ribbons by the men. Stone steers Miss Bald into the briar hedge, trips and sprains his ankle. Randall and Rose are the winners. Rose trotting confidently, guided by Randall's gentle tugs and "gee-ups!" Her head back, showing her pale throat, her knees rising and falling smartly beneath her fresh summer frock, reminding me painfully of days on the beach, plunging into breakers.

At midnight Verschoyle rattles a spoon in a beer mug. Important news, he cries. There is to be a peace conference in the Azores. The squadron is finally returning to base at Bath. Randall has just got engaged to Rose.

SAINT JUDE'S DAY

The squadron left today for the city. The mess cold and sad. Verschoyle, with uncharacteristic generosity, said I could keep the monoplane. There's a 'drome near Tomintoul in the Cairngorms which sounds ideal. Instructed Fielding to fit long-range fuel tanks.

First snows of winter. The Sow & Farrow closed for the season. A shivering Fielding brings news that the monoplane has developed a leak in the glycol system. I order him to work on through the night. I must leave tomorrow.

P.M. Brooding in the mess about Rose, wondering where I went wrong. Stroll outside, find the snow has stopped. *Observation:* when you're alone for any length of time, you develop an annoying inclination to look in mirrors.

A cold sun shines through the empty beeches, casting a blue trellis of shadows on the immaculate white lawn.

Must write to Reggie about the strange temptation to stamp on smooth things. Snow on a lawn, sand at low tide. An overpowering urge to leave a mark?

I stand on the edge, overpoweringly tempted. It's all so perfect, it seems a shame to spoil it. With an obscure sense of pleasure, I yield to the temptation and stride boldly across the unreal surface, my huge footprints thrown into high relief by the candid winter sun. . . .

Bat-Girl!

Arthur's got this amazing tongue. Very long and pointed, pale pink and thin as a knife. He can curl it right round my fingers—very flickery. And, it's wet and warm—not like a cat's, which is rough and dry. I can tell you it doesn't half give me a funny feeling. I lie on my back and he licks away at my hands for hours. He seems quite happy and I get quite carried away sometimes. Shivers all through my body.

Arthur's my bat, of course, and he and I do an "act" together. My aunt Reen runs the show. There's me—Tracy, the bat-girl—and my younger sister Lorraine, snake-girl. I used to be snake-girl but that was when we only had one stall. Then someone gave Reen this big fruit bat and she thought, why not expand? She set up a new stall and here I am, having my fingers licked all day. SEE THE FABULOUS BAT-GIRL! £1,000 IF ANIMAL NOT REAL!!

It sounds quite glamorous, I know, but to be honest it's not much of a job. We do the summer fairground circuit all over England and in the winter go back to Yorkshire where my uncle Ted's got a battery hen-farm. I can tell you that after a few months with those bloody hens I'm aching to be out on the road again. You see, my big problem is that I always need some excitement in my life.

163

Above the pay booth and running the length of the front of the stall there's a big picture of a blond girl with no clothes on, and there's a bat crawling across her body with its wings spread. The booth is new, so the colours are still bright and not too badly chipped and also it's quite warm, which is just as well because it can get quite parky lying around inside a cage all day. I'm not nude, mind you. I wear a swimsuit, one piece, pink with a big bow that holds the two halves of the front together. Arthur hangs upside down from the top of the cage licking my fingers. I dip them in a pot of honey—which he absolutely loves—and he just licks it all off.

Lorraine's set-up is basically the same, except it's not quite so smart. Also, the python does nothing but sleep and I think that what people like about the bat-girl is that they can see the bat is actually alive. He's quite big, is Arthur; he's got a brown furry body about a foot long with nasty-looking claws. And then of course there's his tongue, in and out, slipping all over my fingers. It seems to fascinate some people—they stare for ages. His wings remind me of a leather umbrella.

We'd been in Swindon for a week and had just come down to Oxford for Saint Giles fair. It was my second year in Oxford, though my first as bat-girl, and I wasn't looking forward to it that much. Funny mixture of people you get in Oxford, I always say. There's some right rough ones, don't you believe it. And then there are these student types, they think they're so bloody clever, with their tweed jackets and their haw-haw voices. I remember when I was snake-girl last year, a whole crowd of them had stood and talked about me for twenty minutes as if I wasn't there. Really rude too: "Eoh ai'm convinced she's not alive," one of them says. "Ai'm going to claim my thousand quid." Gets on my wick, that clever-clever lark. Give me the lads from Blackbird Leys any day.

The thing was, I knew there would be extra trouble this year because of the painting Reen had put up of the naked girl. In Lorraine's snake-girl painting she's wearing a bikini, but for some reason Reen decided she'd make bat-girl nude. I said if they're all coming in thinking I'm starkers I want an extra fiver a day for all the aggro I'm going to get. Reen paid up, so I'm not complaining, but my God, you should hear some of the things that get said to me: "Take 'em off, darling" and "Let's have a look then" and that's not the half of it. The problem is this revealing swimsuit Reen makes me wear and the fact that I'm fairly big up top. It's a funny thing about being big-made—blokes seem to think they can say anything to you.

Still, it's water off a duck's back as far as I'm concerned. I'm used to it now so I just lie there and carry on reading my book. I always take a book into the cage because it's a long day and it can get very boring. I read mainly men's books: spies and thrillers, that's what I like. I like a bit of excitement, as I said. That's really why I joined up with Reen soon as I left school. I'm eighteen now and I'm saving up for this dance course in London that I've seen advertised in a magazine. "Felaine la Strade, Ecole de Dance." Five hundred pounds for two months of lessons. You get a diploma, and at the bottom of their prospectus it says: "Many of our graduettes have secured positions in West End shows." Well, I've always been keen on dancing—quite good at it, too—and as I say, you've got to have some ambition and excitement in your life. I mean, look at Lorraine for e.g.: after this summer she's decided to go back to school and retake her O-levels. I ask you—no spirit.

We'd set up in Oxford on the Sunday afternoon. The

site's right in the middle of town on a wide street with trees which is the best thing about it. We had quite a brisk Monday and one woman had screamed when she'd seen Arthur's tongue. A couple of lads from Didcot who I'd met last year tried to chat me up in the evening. They claimed Trevor had said it was okay for me to come out with them. Trevor's my boyfriend; he works on the Whip taking money. I told them to push off. Trev would never let them do that. He's a very jealous sort of guy, is Trev. Actually I'm not speaking to him at the moment. The last night we were in Swindon he showed up when we were taking down the stall with a big wad of cotton-wool Sellotaped to his forearm. I had told him not to get any more tattoos and he'd just gone and done it. He's got enough of them as it is, all over his arms and shoulders, and in any case I've gone right off tattoos. He'd promised not to, so I told him to shove it.

I know we'll get back together, as Trev is really quite strong on me, but I am enjoying not having him hanging around. I'm getting on with my reading too. I finished a complete book on Monday and I've started a new one called *Hell Comes Tomorrow*. It's really exciting.

On Tuesday after lunch, business really tailed off and I was racing through the book when I realised someone had crept into the booth on their own and was staring at me. I looked round and saw a thin bloke with round gold specs who was carrying a briefcase. Only a student, I thought, and went back to my book. Arthur was asleep so I prodded him awake and he hooked his wing-claw over my thumb and gave it a good licking. I thought I'd better do that so's the guy could claim he'd got his money's worth. However, a few minutes later he was still there, so I turned round again and gave him a look—as much to say, that's your lot, mate—and he scurried out pretty sharpish.

But blow me if five minutes later he wasn't back. Just standing and staring. It was beginning to get on my nerves; I couldn't concentrate on my book at all. So I sat up and said: "That's all there is, you know. He doesn't do tricks or anything."

He looked a bit startled. He had quite a nice face and shiny-clean black hair with a middle parting.

"Oh, I'm sorry," he said. "I . . . I find it fascinating, that's all."

Well, I could tell by the way he kept touching the knot of his tie and the look he was giving me that "it" didn't refer to Arthur. He kept on standing there all the same, as if he'd never seen a girl before.

To this day I don't know what made me do it. The heat perhaps—it was muggy and sunny outside. Maybe it was just plain boredom, and he looked so "nice" and decent—the sort that wouldn't say boo to a goose.

When I got the idea, I felt this excited feeling at the bottom of my spine—a sort of electric tingling. So, very slowly—not taking my eyes off him—I leant back on the cushions and pulled out the cord of the bow on my swimsuit. Well, the two front bits kind of fell away— not completely, but he wouldn't miss much. But then I went and laughed. I couldn't help it. The expression on his face—I swear his specs steamed up.

"This what you're after then?" I said between giggles.

You've *never* seen anyone move so fast. Out of the booth like a shot and I didn't stop laughing for ten minutes. Arthur didn't know what'd come over me.

Come five o'clock Reen shuts up the stall for half an hour to let me have a rest, a smoke and get to the lav. I pulled on my jersey and jeans (I keep them folded on a chair beside the cage) and went outside. I lit up a fag and had a good stretch. I normally meet Trev at this time but there was no sign of him on account of our row. But the student who'd been in the booth was there. I felt a bit embarrassed when he saw me and came over.

"Um, I was wondering if you'd like to come and have some tea with me," he said.

Oh, yes? I thought. But then he'd asked so politely, so I said I would.

He took me to his college, which wasn't very far away. They're nice, these colleges that they live in—amazing lawns, not a weed in sight—and very quiet. We went up a little narrow stone staircase to his room. It was quite pleasant—a bit old-looking, though, and very untidy with lots of books and papers. I had a look through his bookshelves when he went out to make the tea but we obviously had different tastes in reading.

We had a few cups of tea and a piece of sponge cake ("Oh, there goes me diet," I said, and would you believe it he blushed). He said his name was Gordon and he told me a bit about his work and asked me some questions about the fair. He was slim and about medium height, was Gordon, and I quite liked him. I kept wondering when he would make his move.

It took him quite a while, but eventually he worked it so we were sitting side by side on the sofa. But then someone knocked on the door and stuck his head into the room. It was another guy with specs and he said,

"*Oh!* Jesus . . . sorry, Gord. Didn't know you had company," and popped out again. Gordon had leapt to his feet and looked more embarrassed than ever. I've never known anyone quite like Gordon for going red, honestly. Anyway, I put him out of his misery and told him I had to get back.

On the way to the booth he asked if he could meet me when the fair shut down. I told him we had to pack up tonight, as we were setting up in Northampton to-morrow. He looked disappointed at this but said he'd still like to come and say goodbye. That was fine by me, I said. He had nice manners, had Gordon. He hadn't once mentioned our little episode with the swimsuit.

Gordon was waiting for me at eleven o'clock when the fair began to shut down. I was carrying Arthur in a small parrot's cage. I was a bit worried in case Trev might have shown up but there was no sign of him. I told Gordon he could carry Arthur to Reen's car, which was parked some way off. Gordon said he knew a short cut.

We walked through the fair. As usual Gordon wasn't saying much. Stalls were coming down and the big lor-ries were backing slowly along the street. A few groups of young kids hung round watching it all. The ground was covered in litter: tickets, squashed toffee apples and bits of coloured paper and burst balloons. It always makes me a bit sad when the fair comes down so I just walked along quietly beside Gordon.

We turned up this narrow alley that led between two of the old colleges. It was dark, as there was only one street light and huge black chestnut trees hung over us. It felt a bit spooky so I linked my arm through Gor-don's and you'd have thought I'd stabbed him in the back. His knee banged into Arthur's cage and I could hear Arthur scrabbling around trying to keep his grip.

"Hold on a sec, Gordon," I said. "Put Arthur down for a moment. Let him get settled."

Gordon put the cage on the ground and I knelt down to peer in at Arthur. Gordon knelt down, too, and muttered something about Arthur being a fascinating creature.

We got up together and I thought, poor sod, and leant up against him ever so slightly. He put his arms round

me and we sort of stood there for a while. I could feel
him all shivery and excited and I ran my hands through
his hair. It felt lovely.

The next thing I knew he wasn't there. He'd been torn
out of my arms and I gave a little scream when I saw it
was Trev. Trev, who had him by the back of his jacket
and was spinning him round and round. Then he let
him go and Gordon careered into the wall with an awful thump that sent his specs flying to the ground.

Trev stood in front of him swearing and spitting.
"Okay Trace," he shouted over his shoulder at me.
"Where do I give it him first. You tell me, Trace."

Christ, really, Trev looked amazing. He's a big lad and
he had tight black jeans on and a white T-shirt with
KUNG-FU written on it. His chest was heaving up and
down and his hair was sort of wild.

Gordon leant up against the wall half-crumpled, as if
he'd been pinned onto it. He didn't stand a chance.

I didn't say anything though. Gordon must have seen
me standing there all excited because he tried to get to
his feet. Trev gave him a push and he fell onto the
ground.

"Don't boot him, Trev," I yelled, because I could see
that was what he was about to do. "Get his specs, go on,
get his specs."

Then Trev saw Gordon's specs on the ground and
he just stamped on them. Bang. Once. Like he was
squashing a beetle crawling across the floor. Then he
kicked them up the alley.

He turned and looked at me. "See you at the car, girl,"
he says, all harsh and angry. "Bloody pronto." And he
walks off just like that.

I felt my heart was going to punch itself out of my
rib cage. My head felt all light. He can do that to me,
can Trev. Amazing sort of bloke.

I went and got Gordon's spectacles. There was no glass in them and they were badly bent. When I handed them back to him I could see the red marks they had made on his nose. His eyes were all watery and blank-looking.

"Sorry, Gordon," I said. "But it was better that he done your specs. He's mean, is Trevor, and he's my boy-friend."

Gordon nodded without saying anything and pushed his glasses into his pocket. I helped him up and straightened out his jacket. There didn't seem to be much to say. Trevor must have seen us at the stall and followed.

"I'd better go," I said. Trev would be waiting, I knew. I picked up Arthur and began to walk off.

"Tracy," I heard Gordon wheeze. "Just a moment."

I went back to him. He did look quite different without his glasses—sort of ordinary, not so intelligent.

"Next year," he said. "Will you be back next year?"

I was astonished. "I don't know," I said. "Why?"

"I thought . . ." he began to say. Then: "It's just that I shall be here." Then he gave a grim little laugh. "In fact I shall probably die here."

That made me feel all sorry for him—he had no excitement in his life apart from me—and so I decided not to tell him about Felaine la Strade and the Ecole de Dance. Better to let him dream a bit. *He* might be here still, but there was no way you'd catch me as bat-girl again next year, no chance. I'd be in London, the big smoke, a dancer or something.

But I reached out and patted Gordon's arm. "Don't worry," I said. "Me and Arthur'll be back. We'll have tea again. See you next year." Then I turned away and walked back up the alley to where I knew Trev would be waiting. Just before I turned the corner I looked back, and there was Gordon, standing there—he hadn't moved an inch—staring at me, just staring at me like the first time he had come into the booth. It still gave me the shivers. He was quite a nice guy, was Gordon. It was a pity really—yes, the whole thing was a pity.

Love Hurts

10 August 1973

It was sometime in the hot freedom of July that I introduced Cherylle to Lamar. I think it was at my delayed welcoming party that AOD were throwing. Cherylle was an out of work actress who rented the apartment below mine with two other girls. Quite spontaneously I had decided to invite one of them along—I had as yet made no friends since arriving here from England and felt I needed an ally of sorts at this gathering of off-duty American executives and their brittle, frosted wives. Cherylle was the only girl at home when I knocked on the apartment door. Such are the tricks time plays. She is marrying Lamar tomorrow.

Cherylle: tall, bony, a shock of wild blond hair. Twenty-five years old? Typically Californian flawless skin. I find her an oddly attractive girl without really being able to say why—a product of the curious vectors of a face: the arc of an eyebrow, the prominence of a cheekbone. There is a simmering feral gleam in her gaze, a sense of coiled, ticking energy within her which only truly strikes you on a third or fourth meeting.

Lamar, however, claims he spotted it instantly and it was this he found irresistibly attractive. I should say that Lamar has since become my closest friend out here on the Coast. Looking back through my diary I see I first described him as "a characteristically butch American businessman. Late thirties, handsome, tanned and stocky. Tough as a hill. Self-confidence surrounds him like a force field. The youngest vice-president in the company, responsible for sales and marketing. They say AOD will be his before the decade's out." Now that I know him I would say that this is only partially true. Lamar still exudes this brash ease but it's something of a façade. He is no typical VP; he works hard at his job because that is all his background and education have trained him to do. He has his idiosyncrasies and I find him both stimulating and sad.

For example, the fact that I write—albeit commercially—for a living has prompted him to attack the cultural lacunae in his life with the same vigour he applies to chase after contracts. He sees me as some sort of intellectual guru, a source to be tapped and exploited. Quite early on in our friendship he suggested we read through Shakespeare together "because they say he's the best." To feed this new enthusiasm I gave him reading lists and drew up programmes for his educational self-improvement. He proved to be a sensitive and intelligent student, surprisingly perceptive. He would question me so endlessly I felt exhausted, victim of some nightmare seminar, dizzy from the rapacity with which he plundered my brain.

His friendship with Cherylle did not affect the growth of our own. Indeed the three of us often went out together. And as the two of them became swiftly more infatuated, my presence paradoxically seemed all the more essential. I became the talisman of their affair, as if they needed the constant reassuring presence of the catalyst that had started the reaction off.

I have, however, tried to talk to Lamar about the wisdom of this wedding—gently councilled delay. Cherylle is an incandescent but mercurial character, wayward and, I suspect, deeply uncertain of herself. But Lamar will not listen. He is in love, he insists, wholly in love for the first time in his life.

11 August 1973
The wedding. Lamar and Cherylle get riotously drunk. At the civic hall Cherylle arrived in thigh-length suede boots, jeans and a bright-yellow windcheater. She dresses in a bizarre series of fashions—sometimes glaring lack of taste, sometimes shining with demure chicness. Hardly the wife for a rising vice-president, I would have thought, but Lamar seems to accept her extravagances with a wide-eyed, ingenuous thrill.

Now I know her better I take Cherylle's lurid anthology of styles to be evidence of a chronic insecurity in her personality. She teeters on the brink of moods with the practised equilibrium of the perennially schizoid. Lamar, somehow, responds to this. His marriage to Cherylle is the one publicly irrational event in his entirely ordered life. He told me once he understood her perfectly, could predict her moves and responses with a Pavlovian confidence. He underestimates Cherylle, I think, and I am a little concerned. He has never displayed such verve and elation, but this is no Platonic union of opposites. Lamar's efficient diurnal parade has broken up to join Cherylle's Mardi Gras—and it likes the headlong pace.

14 August 1973
Working steadily for the last two days in the beach house. Windless, lustrous weather. Postcard from Lamar and Cherylle honeymooning in Mexico. Lamar's neat printed script overlaid at the foot of the card by some illegible felt-tip scrawl from Cherylle. Lamar says

I would "love the art." Is he being ironic? I suspect it's a sop to our abandoned educational sessions—maybe he's feeling guilty. They didn't stand much chance against the potent lure of Cherylle's callow, hard-edged embrace.

18 August 1973

Lamar and Cherylle returned this morning, tanned and restless, deeply bored by Mexico. They stayed for lunch. Their evident intoxication with each other is off-putting, to say the least. Lamar was unshaven and in a T-shirt. There were bags under his eyes. I've never seen him like this.

Their self-absorption has its curious aspects too. Judging from the hints Lamar dropped about their days in Mexico, it seems that it only functions non-destructively when observed by a third party. He alluded to uncouth nights of violent, manic rows and equally violent and manic reconciliations. He calls it "kamikaze love" and describes it as a mixture of "laughter and pistol shots"—which is quite good for Lamar. He claims he finds it entirely invigorating.

I suspect I am to be enrolled as resident third party: token voyeur of their lambent encounters. I'm not sure I welcome the role; I sense this self-destruct mechanism poised inside Cherylle and it makes me uncomfortable. For example, she was quiet and affectionate all afternoon; then she swam worryingly far out to sea. "Trying for Catalina Island" was all she said when she returned exhausted. They left about eight in the evening heading for some dim bar on the Strip.

19 August 1973

To the downtown offices of AOD to present the first draft of my package. Looked in on Lamar but his office was empty. His secretary said you could never tell when he'd be in these days. Over lunch with some of his colleagues I found that Cherylle was the prime topic of conversation. There's a certain smug satisfaction evinced over the changes she's wrought in Lamar; normally the paradigm of the totally committed company man, he now delegates more and more, and his faultless punctuality has degenerated to amnesiac randomness.

23 August 1973

Drove up the coast with Lamar and Cherylle in their new car, a preposterously large white Buick convertible. An unusual vernal, sappy feel to the day—all the colours seem unfledged and new. Cherylle was at her most entrancing, telling us stories of her attempts to break into the movies. Looking at Lamar, I see devotion lodged in every feature. He seems not to listen to her words, but rather watches her forming them—noting every smile, eye gleam, pout and hair-toss like some fervent anthropologist.

On the beach Cherylle changed into a skimpy scarlet bikini and we took photographs of each other. Lamar had given her an expensive camera as a present and we played with its delayed exposure device, taking endless reels of the three of us in absurd vaudevillian poses, throughout which Cherylle flirted shamelessly with me. Lamar—a little subdued, I thought—later moved up to the dunes with the telephoto lens. I saw him up there, obsessively sniping shots of her as she oiled herself and sunbathed.

When we got back home I found myself drained and exhausted from the sun and the fervid high spirits. Lamar and Cherylle wanted me to come and "cruise bars." Lately their favourite pastime, it lasts all night—an intoxicating carnival snaking through the seamier side of the city. I begged off—I scarcely had the energy for a shower. I don't know how they can keep this pace up.

4 September 1973

Lamar phoned and asked in a morose voice if he could come round and have a talk. Alone. I hadn't seen him or Cherylle since that day at the beach and I wondered what was going on. He looked something like his old self—neater, back in a suit. Apparently word had come down from the higher echelons that the honeymoon was over. The postures of his body, however, struck attitudes of despair and gloom. Things were not going well. Cherylle hated to be on her own now that he had to be regularly at work. On one of their bar cruises they had met a young hippie-actor friend of Cherylle. He had stayed the night and was still there. "He's a remarkable sort of guy," Lamar insisted, unconvincingly. "Only I wish he and Cherylle didn't laugh so much together." Kick him out, I advised. No, Lamar said, no. Cherylle wouldn't like that. My heart went out to him. We sat on and talked a bit longer, Lamar feigning unconcern, but with his strong shoulders slumped, his kamikaze love in a screaming death dive, the end of his fabulous amours, his brief bright horizon dimmed by valedictory clouds.

11 September 1973

I arrived home at the beach house this evening to find Lamar there waiting. I knew from his blank eyes Cherylle had gone. "Took the white Buick," Lamar said, his voice numbly monotone, "and everything in the house they could hock. No note, nothing."

I poured him a drink. She was young, I said, headstrong. She'd be back soon, to apologise, wanting to be forgiven. As he left, Lamar gripped my arm fiercely. "You know," he said evenly, "I can't face it. If she doesn't come back." I reassured him. I'd lay odds I said—five days, ten at the most. Wait until the money ran out, the binge was over.

29 September 1973
Lamar looks pale and sick. He hardly sleeps, he says. He has hired a private detective to look for Cherylle. Apparently everyone at work has been most under-standing. Now that Cherylle has been away for three weeks, sympathetic consolation has turned to worldly reasoning. You're better off without her, his colleagues declare with firm logic. Think of your career—be ob-jective—did she *really* fit in? Yeah, anyone could see there was something unstable there. Hell, Lamar, they said, she's done you a *favour*.

But Lamar, it was obvious, would never agree. He spent more and more time at my place tirelessly rerun-ning the scenario of his brief courtship and marriage as if he were trying to unlock some code the memories contained. A bleak dawn often broke on these discon-solate monologues: me in a half-doze; Lamar, his head in his hands, eyes staring emptily out to sea as if searching the sombre distance for an answer.

5 October 1973
10.30 P.M. A call from Cherylle. Would I meet her in the forecourt of a filling station not far from my house. Ah, I thought, I am about to be enrolled as mediator. However, Cherylle was proud and unrepentant. The Buick was parked at the kerb. Her boyfriend leaned against it just out of earshot. Cherylle looked more wild and unkempt. She gave me the keys to the car and an envelope of money. "Tell him to keep away," she said. "I owe him nothing now." I was puzzled and a little an-gry. "What about an explanation?" I said. "Why did you do it?" She laughed. "Nobody could take that kind of a

relationship," she said. "I was like some kind of dog, a
pet dog. It would have killed me."

When I got home I called Lamar and told him about
our meeting. He came right over. When he saw the car
and the money he broke down for the first time. I took
him home, told him to get some sleep and said I'd be
round the next day. He behaved like the victim of some
appalling accident, a focal point for massive stresses.

14 October 1973

Much of my spare time over the last few days has been
spent with Lamar. Our conversation on all other topics
except Cherylle is desultory and half-hearted. There has
been no further word from her.

Lamar is driven on remorselessly by his obsession.
Now that her presence has been removed from him he
hoards items of her clothing like religious treasures, the
banal relics of a consumer saint. He carries around with
him a cheap Zippo lighter engraved with her name, and
a disposable powder compact which he is forever
touching and examining like some demented votary.

We drive around at night to the bars they visited, in
the vague hope of spotting her. Every distant blonde is
excitedly approached until the lack of resemblance becomes clear. His moods on these occasions oscillate
wildly, a leaping seismograph of elation and despair.

One day we drove back to the beach we had visited.
Lamar sat in what he felt was the exact spot, raking the
sand with his fingers like an insane archaeologist, finding only the cellophane wrapper of a cigarette pack and
the plastic top of a tube of sun oil. Then two nights ago
he asked me to come with him to Lake Folsom, where
he and Cherylle had spent a weekend. We wandered
aimlessly through the resort complex and then went
down to the marina. There, Lamar stopped to talk to

an old boatman who had rented them a cruiser for the day. He said he remembered Cherylle and asked for her. When Lamar told him what had happened he spat bitterly into the lake. He scrutinised the ripples he had caused for a few seconds and then said, "Yeah. I seen 'em all." Then he paused. "I seen 'em all here," he went on. "Fame, fornication and tears. That's all there is."

Lamar seemed profoundly affected by this piece of folk-wisdom and repeated the remark approvingly to himself several times on the journey home.

17 October 1973

A surprise invitation to Lamar's for dinner. There were just the two of us. He tells me that after considerable thought he has eventually filed for divorce. He seems calmer but the brimming self-assurance that was there has not returned. The old solidity, too, seems a thing of the past; there is a slight lack of ease—a convalescent's awkwardness—in his movements. After dinner he brought out all the shiny photos he had taken of Cherylle. He flicked through them once and then burnt them. He pointed to a slowly curling Kodachrome. "Cherylle, that day at the beach . . . remember the swimsuit?" Then he smiled, embarrassed. "I'm sorry," he said. "I know it's absurdly melodramatic, but at least I feel it's over now."

We went out later to buy some cigarettes. On our way back we saw a girl in a yellow window crying over a typewriter. "Think Cherylle's crying for me?" he asked harshly. I said that she might be. "No, she's not," he said firmly. "Not Cherylle."

23 October 1973

I was woken early this morning by the police. They said Lamar wanted me. Outside, he sat in the back seat

of a police car. "They've found her," he said. "They want
me to identify. Will you come with me?"

Cherylle's decomposing body had been found in a
shack at an abandoned dude ranch out in the desert near
a place called Hi Vista. There was no sign of the hippie-actor friend. Apparently it had all the indications
of a half-fulfilled suicide pact. There was a note with
both their signatures, but the police suspected that after
Cherylle had pulled the trigger her lover had pan-
icked, had second thoughts about joining her and had
fled.

The deep irony was not lost on Lamar. He stood un-
movingly as the policeman pulled back the blanket and
there was only a slight huskiness in his voice as he iden-
tified her body.

2 November 1973

Lamar has just moved back to his flat. He had been
staying with me since the inquest. The hippie has still
not been tracked down. Lamar has been a moody and
taciturn companion, not surprisingly, but he is not the
broken man I expected him to be. There is a kind of
fatalistic resignation about him, he talks less obsessively
about Cherylle and I'm glad to say seems to have abandoned his mementoes. However, it has to be said that
he is nothing like the person he was a few short months
ago and he told me yesterday he planned to resign from
the company. He keeps saying that Cherylle couldn't
have been happy, so it was just as well that she ended
it all. "She couldn't have been happy," he will say. "Not
Cherylle. If she couldn't be happy with me, how could
she possibly be happy with anybody else?" To Lamar's
numbed brain the logic of that statement appears in-
controvertible.

8 November 1973

A dull smog-shrouded day of rain. By mistake the police forwarded on Cherylle's personal possessions to my house, assuming Lamar was still staying here. A patrol car dropped them off early in the evening and I said I would make sure Lamar got them. There was a nylon suitcase full of crumpled clothes and a plastic bag of loose items. I laid them on the kitchen table and thought sadly of Cherylle. Cherylle, in her satin pants . . . her orange lips, her white-blond hair. And now? A few grubby clothes, a wooden hairbrush, sunglasses, a Mexican purse, a charm, a powder compact and a Zippo lighter with her name engraved on it . . .

I finally caught up with Lamar at a burger dinette down on the seafront not far from his apartment. It was still raining heavily. He sat at a table in the window surrounded by wax-paper wrappers and empty bottles of beer, gazing out at the passing trucks on the coast highway. A red tail-light glow lit his eyes.

I placed the Zippo and the compact in front of him on the table. "Why did you do it?" I asked. He hardly looked surprised. He gave a momentary start before resuming his scrutiny of the passing traffic.

"They were hers," he said dully. "I didn't want them any more so I just put them back in her bag."

"But why, Lamar? Why?" His woodenness infuriated me. "Why Cherylle?"

He looked at me as though I'd asked a stupid question. "She wasn't ever coming back, you know? But I found out where she was. I begged her on my knees to come home. But that hippie wouldn't let her go. I tried to buy him off, but he wasn't interested. And I couldn't let her leave me for someone like that—for anyone. I had to do it, so I set it up that way."

"What about him? The hippie?"

"Oh, he's out there in the desert. No one's going to find him in a long time."

Lamar smiled a bitter smile and traced a pattern in the wet Formica round his beer bottle. A young Hispanic waitress approached for my order, carrying her boredom like a rucksack. I waved her away. I wanted to get out of this melancholy bar with its flickering neon and clouded chrome.

I had reached the door when I felt his hand on my shoulder.

"You can tell them if you like. I don't care." He looked at me tiredly.

I felt my voice thick in my throat. "Just tell me one thing," I said. "I want to know how you feel now. Feel tough, Lamar? Feel noble? Come on, what's it like, Lamar?"

He shrugged. "Remember that play we read once? 'I'll sacrifice the lamb that I do love'? That's how it is, you know? It's like the song says—love hurts. It gets to hurt you so much you've got to do something about it."

It was all the explanation I would ever get. He stood in the doorway and watched me walk to my car. Tyres swishing on the wet tarmac, the road shiny like vinyl, the rain slicking down his short hair. As I drove off I could see him in the rear mirror, still standing there, a lurid burger sign smoking above his head. I never saw him again.

The Coup

Isaac knocked at his door at half past three in the morning. It took Morgan a few minutes to wake up; then he washed, shaved and put on his light-weight tropical suit. He was going home.

The verandah was cluttered with the trunks and packing cases that were being shipped back to England separately by sea. Morgan ate his breakfast among them in a mood of quite pleasant melancholy. He gazed across the empty sitting room and at the bare walls of his bungalow and thought about the three years he had spent in this stinking sweaty country. Three rotting years. Christ.

He was still thinking about how much he wouldn't miss the place when the car from the High Commission arrived at half past four. Morgan registered a twinge of annoyance when he saw that instead of the air-conditioned Mercedes he'd requested, he'd been issued with a cream Ford Consul. It was three and a half hours from Nkongsamba to the capital by road; three and a half hours of switchbacked, pot-holed hell through dense rain forest. It seemed that his last hours in this wretched country were destined to be spent in the same perspiring, itching agony that so coloured his memories of the past three years. Typical of the bloody High Commis-

sioner, thought Morgan, not bloody important enough
for the Merc. Trust the little asthmatic bureaucrat to
notice his transport application. He'd wanted the Merc
desperately; to strap-hang in air-conditioned comfort,
the Union Jack cracking on the bonnet. Go out in style—
that had been the plan. He looked critically at the Consul; it needed a clean and one hub cap was missing, *and*
they'd given him that imbecilic driver Peter. Morgan
rolled his eyes heavenwards. He couldn't wait to leave.

He said goodbye to Isaac, and Moses his cook, and
Moses' young wife Abigail, who helped with the washing and ironing. He'd given them all a sizeable farewell
dash the previous evening and he noticed they were
smiling hugely as they energetically pumped his hands.
Bloody gang of Old Testament refugees, he thought,
slightly put out at the absence of any sadness or solem-
nity; they'd never had it so good. He cast his eye fondly
over Abigail's plump, sleek body. Yes, he'd miss the
women, he admitted, and the beer.

It was still quite black outside and a couple of toads
burped at each other in the darkness of the garden as
he eased himself onto the shiny plastic rear seat, gave
a final wave, and told Peter to get going. They sped off
through the deserted roads of the commercial reser-
vation and passed quickly through the narrow empty
streets of Nkongsamba before striking what was laugh-
ingly known as the transnational highway.

This particular road was a crumbling two-lane tar-
macadam death trap that meandered through the jungle between Nkongsamba and the capital. A skilfully
designed route of blind corners, uncambered Z-bends
and savage gradients, it annually claimed hundreds of
lives as the worst drivers in the world sought to nego-
tiate its bizarre geometry. The small hours of the
morning were the only time when it was anything like

safe to travel—hence Morgan's early rise, even though his plane left at half past eleven.

As a citron light spread over the jungle, Morgan reflected that they hadn't made such bad progress. With the windows wound full down the speeding car had been filled with a cool breeze and Morgan barely sweated at all. As expected, the roads had been quiet. They had passed the still-guttering remains of a crashed petrol tanker and once had been forced off the road by a criminally overloaded articulated lorry, its two huge trailers towering with sacks of groundnuts, as its bonus-hunting driver, high on kolanuts, barrelled down the middle of the road en route for the capital and its busy port.

All in all a remarkably uneventful journey, thought Morgan as they raced through a town called Shagamu, which marked the halfway stage. But then it was only a matter of a few miles farther on, the sun's heat concentrating, Morgan's buttocks and the backs of his ample thighs beginning to chafe and fret on the plastic seats, that they had a puncture. The car veered suddenly, Morgan threw up his arms, Peter shouted "Good Lord!" and he pulled onto the laterite verge.

After the steady rumble of their passage on the tarmac, it was very quiet. The road stretched empty before and behind them, the avenue of jungle rearing up on either side like high green walls.

Peter got out and looked at the tyre, sucking in air through the prodigious gaps in his teeth. He grinned.

"Dis be poncture, sah," he explained through the window.

Morgan didn't budge. "Well, bloody fix it then," he growled. "I've got a plane to catch, you know."

Peter went round to the back of the car and threw open the boot. Morgan sat scowling, the absence of breeze through the car windows reminding him pointedly of the high humidity and the unrelenting heat of the early morning sun. He had a sudden agonising itch on his perineum. He scratched at it furiously.

Then Peter was back at the window.

"Ah-ah! Sah, dey never give us one spear."

"Spear? Spear? What bloody spear?"

"Spear tyre, sah. Dere is no spear tyre for boot."

Morgan climbed out of the car swearing. Sure enough, no spare. He felt an intolerable explosive frustration building up in him. This bloody country just wasn't going to give up, was it? Oh, no, far too much to expect to catch a plane unhindered. He gazed wildly around at the green jungle before telling himself to calm down.

"You'd better take the wheel back to Shagamu." He thrust some notes into Peter's hand. "Try and get it fixed. And hurry!"

Peter jacked up the Consul, removed the wheel and trundled it back down the road to Shagamu. It was too hot to sit in the car, so Morgan crouched on the verge in what little shade it offered and watched the sun climb the sky.

A few cars whizzed past but nobody stopped. The highway, Morgan grimly noted, was particularly quiet today.

Two and a half hours later, Peter returned with a repaired and newly inflated tyre. It took another ten minutes to replace it before they were on their way once more. Morgan's plane was due to leave in just over an hour. They would never make it. His face was taut and expressionless as they roared down the road to the airport.

The airport was situated on flat land about ten miles from the capital and was quite cut off, surrounded by a large light-industrial estate. As they drove past the small factories, freight depots and vehicle pools. Morgan again commented on the lack of traffic; everybody seemed to be staying away. Small groups of people gathered in the villages at the roadside and stared curiously at the cream Consul as it went by. Probably some bloody holiday, reasoned Morgan thankfully as he saw the signposts directing them to the airport. At least something was working in his favour.

Soon he saw the familiar roadside billboards advertising airlines and the exotic places they visited, and Morgan felt the first thrill of excitement at the thought of flying off home; the well-modulated chill of the aircraft, the crisp stewardesses and the duty-free liquor. He was straightening his tie as they rounded a corner and almost ran down a road-block.

The road-block consisted of three fifty-gallon oil drums surmounted by planks of wood. Parked to one side was a chubby armoured car, surrounded by at least two dozen soldiers wearing camouflage uniforms and armed with sub-machine-guns with sickle-shaped magazines.

Morgan stared in open-mouthed astonishment about him and at the airport buildings two hundred yards ahead. Four huge tanks were parked in front of the arrivals hall. Morgan noticed with alarm that several of the soldiers had levelled their guns at the car. Peter's face was positively grey with fear. A young officer approached with a red cockade in his peaked cap. He politely asked Morgan to get out and produce his documents.

"What's going on?" Morgan asked impatiently. "Is this some kind of an exercise? Terrorists? Or what? Look here"—he pointed to his identity card—"I'm a member of the British diplomatic corps and I've got a plane to catch."

The young officer returned the documents.

"This airport is now under the command of the military government . . ." he began, as if reading prompt-cards behind Morgan's head.

"What military government?" Morgan interrupted; then, as realisation dawned: "Oh, no. Oh, my God, no. A coup—it's a coup. Don't tell me. That's all I need, a bloody *coup*." He raised his right hand to his forehead in an unconsciously dramatic gesture of despair. He felt he was getting a migraine. A bad one.

Just then a BOAC staff car drove up from the airport buildings and a harassed official got out. After some conferring with the young officer he hurried over to Morgan.

"What on earth are you doing here, man?" he asked irritatedly. "Haven't you heard about the coup? This place has been like an armed camp since six o'clock this morning."

Morgan explained about his early start and the puncture. "Listen," he went on agitatedly, "my plane. Have I missed my plane? When can I get out of here?"

"Sorry, old chap. The last plane left here at midnight. The airport's closed to civil traffic. As you can see, there's not a thing here. This is what usually happens, I believe. Nobody flies in or out for a few days until things have sorted themselves out. You know, until the radio blackout's lifted, the fighting stops and the new government's officially recognised."

"But look here," Morgan insisted, "I'm from the Commission at Nkongsamba. I've got diplomatic immunity, all that sort of stuff."

"I'm afraid that doesn't carry any weight at all at the moment," said the airlines official in an annoyingly good-humoured manner. "Britain hasn't recognised the new government yet. I'd hang on for a few days before you start claiming any privileges."

"Hang on! Good God, man, where do you suggest I hang on?"

"Well, you can't get back to Nkongsamba. They'll have road-blocks on the highway now, for sure. And there's a twenty-four-hour curfew on in the capital as well. So if I were you, I'd go to the airport hotel down the road. Show them your ticket. I suppose you're in our care now, after a fashion, and they'll bill the airline. I should think they'll be glad of the custom. Everyone else has kept well away, stayed at home. In fact you're the only person who's turned up to catch a flight today. I suppose you were just unlucky."

Morgan turned away. Unlucky. Just unlucky. Story of his life. He climbed morosely into the car and told Peter to take him to the airport hotel. Peter backed up with alacrity and they drove off.

The airport hotel was a mile away. They were stopped by a patrol on the road and Morgan again explained his predicament, flourishing his passport and ticket. He was sunk in a profound depression; the final bizarre revenge of a hostile country. The magnitude of his ill-fortune left him feeling weak and exhausted.

Morgan had stayed at the airport hotel several times before. He remembered it as a lively, cosmopolitan place with two restaurants, several bars, an Olympic-sized swimming pool and a small casino. It was usually populated by a mixed crowd of jet-lagged transit passengers, air-crew and stewardesses and a somewhat raffish and frontier collection of bush-charter pilots, oil company troubleshooters and indeterminate tanned and brassy females whom Morgan imaginatively took to be the mistresses of African politicians, part-time night-club singers, croupiers, hostesses, expensive whores and bored wives. It was as close as Morgan ever came to being a member of the Jet Set and a stay there always

made him feel vaguely mysterious and highly sexed. As
they approached, he recalled how only last year he had
almost successfully bedded a strong-shouldered female
helicopter pilot, and his heart thumped in anticipation.
Every cloud, he reminded himself, silver lining and all
that. That had to be the one consolation of a truly awful day.

The airport hotel was large. A low-slung old colonial
edifice at the centre was lined by shaded concrete path-
ways to more modern bedroom blocks, the pool, the
hairdressing salon and the other amenities. As they
swept up the drive, Morgan looked about him with
something approaching eagerness.

The large car-park, however, was unsettlingly empty,
and Morgan noticed that the familiar troupe of hawk-
ers who spread their thorn carvings, their ithyphallic
ebony statuary and ropes of ceramic beads on the steps
up to the front door were absent. Also there was an
unnatural hush and tranquillity in the foyer, as if
Morgan had arrived at the dead of night rather than
midday. Sitting on squeaky cane chairs in front of the
reception desk were two bored soldiers with small
aluminum machine pistols in their laps. The clerk behind the long desk was asleep, his head resting on the
register. One of the soldiers shook him awake and as
Morgan signed in he noticed that only a few names were
registered along with his own.

"Are you busy?" he asked with faint hope.

The receptionist smiled. "Oh, no, sah. Everybody
gone. Only eight people staying since last night. No
planes," he added, "no guests."

An aged bellhop with bare feet and a faded blue uniform showed Morgan to his room in one of the new
blocks. Morgan was glad to find the air-conditioning still
functioned.

The day's frustrations were not over. Morgan tried

to phone the Commission in Nkongsamba but was informed that all the lines had been closed down by the army. He then went back outside and instructed Peter—who had elected to stay and live in the car in the car-park—to drive to the embassy in the capital and report Morgan's plight.

Peter shook his head with a convincing display of bitter disappointment.

"You can never go dere," he lamented. "Dey done build one big road-block for here," he gestured at a point a few yards up from the end of the hotel drive. "Plenty soldier. Dey are never lettin' you pass."

So that was it. Morgan looked at his watch. By rights he should be high over Europe now, a stewardess handing him his meal on a tray, an hour or so from an early evening touchdown at Heathrow Airport. Instead he was marooned in a deserted hotel complex while a military coup raged outside the gate.

He walked sadly back to his room through the afternoon heat. Lizards basked on stones in the sun, idly doing press-ups as he approached, reverting to glazed immobility once more as he walked on by. To his left he saw the tall diving board of the swimming pool, and some asterisks of light flashed off the blue water he could glimpse through the perforated concrete screen that surrounded the pool area. Normally it would be lively with bathers, the bars crowded with sun-reddened guests, the nearby tennis courts resounding to the pock-pock of couples rallying. Where were the other people who were staying here? Morgan wondered. What were they like? He felt like some mad dictator, or eccentric millionaire recluse, alone in an entire multi-bedroom block with only his taciturn guards for company.

His second question was answered that evening when he went down to the restaurant. There was a table of four Syrians or Lebanese men, and an ancient, wrinkled American couple. The Lebanese ignored him; the Americans said, "Hello, there," and looked anxious to exchange grumbles about their common predicament. Morgan sat as far away as he could. Pretend nothing has happened, he told himself; as soon as we start behaving like victims of a siege—sharing resources, privations and anecdotes—this enforced stay really will become a nightmare.

He was well into his rather firm avocado when the eighth guest arrived. If he had been asked to speculate, unseen, on his or her identity, Morgan—knowing his luck—would have laid long odds on the eighth guest being a nun, an overweight salesman or moustachioed spinster. He was surprised then, and almost enchanted when a young woman entered wearing the dark-blue skirt and white blouse of BOAC. She was quite pretty, too, Morgan assessed, his avocado untended, as he watched her sway through the empty tables to her seat close to the Americans.

For a minute or so Morgan's heartbeat seemed to echo rather loudly in his chest as, more surreptitiously, he scrutinised the girl. "Girl" was perhaps a little too kind. She looked to be well into her thirties, that short blond hair certainly dyed, a slightly predatory air about her features due to the rather hooked nose, the liberally applied cosmetics, and lines that ran from the corners of her nostrils to the ends of her thin orange lips. She had amazingly long painted nails that matched the colour of her lipstick.

For the first time that day Morgan's spirits were lifted. Something about her—the dark eye-shadow, her tan against the white cotton of her blouse—reminded him of the brisk sexual allure of the helicopter pilot of the year before. He passed the rest of the meal in a pleasantly absorbing miasma of sexual fantasy.

Fantasy was all he had to content himself with, however, as the girl appeared to return to her room directly after dinner. Morgan drank a couple of whiskies in the bar but was driven out by the increasingly clamorous garrulity of the four Lebanese, who played bridge with a quite un-English fervour and intensity. The American couple tried to befriend him once again but Morgan repelled their polite "Say, do you have any idea where we can change some dollars?" with a rush of eyebrow-jerking, shoulder-shrugging pseudo French: "Ah, *desolé*, haw . . . euh, *je vous ne comprendre, non? Oui? Disdonc*, eur, bof, *vous savez* haha *parler pas Anglais.* Mmm?" They wandered off with an air of baffled resignation.

The next morning, Morgan looked out of his fifth-floor window. From this height he commanded a considerable view of the hotel area. He could see Peter pissing into a bush on the edge of the car-park. A military jeep was pulled up in front of the central building. Over to his left and partially obscured by a clump of trees he could see the swimming pool: a static blue slab surrounded by grey concrete and ranks of empty lounging chairs. Then, as he watched, a small figure came into his line of vision. It was the stewardess, wearing what looked like a tiny yellow bikini. She jumped into the pool and swam round. Morgan watched dry-mouthed as she clambered dripping up the steps and fingered free the sodden material of her briefs, which had become wedged in the cleft between her buttocks. Morgan turned from the window and rummaged in his suitcase for his swimming trunks.

Morgan was not proud of the state he had allowed his body to get into. Always what his mother had called "a big lad," he had assiduously developed at university a beer-gut which never disappeared and indeed had since expanded like some soft subcutaneous parasite around the sides of his torso, padding his back and swelling his already considerable buttocks and thighs. He could have done something about it once, he supposed as he stood in front of the full-length bathroom mirror; there was nothing he could do about his balding head, but the recent addition of a thick Zapata moustache had effected some positive transformation of his appearance. A straggling line of pale brown hair ran straight down from his throat, between his worryingly plump breasts, to disappear beneath the waistband of his capacious trunks. "Not a pretty sight," a girlfriend had once remarked on observing him as he stumbled—soap-blind—from the shower, groping for a towel. Well, it was too late now, he concluded, inflating his chest and trying to suck in his stomach. In a suit he fancied he looked merely beefy; but this was another trouble with tropical climes: the terrible exposure that resulted through the regular need to shed as much clothing as possible.

Still, he felt quite good as he strolled down the walkway towards the pool, a carefully slung towel modestly covering his shuddering paps. A few more soldiers lounged by the hotel entrance, and the sun beat down from a perfectly blue sky. The enforced, unreal isolation and the unsettling threat of casually sported arms he found strangely invigorating, as if the deserted hotel complex were infused with a lurking wayward sexuality only waiting to be sprung from cover.

Morgan spread his towel a polite few chairs away from the girl. She was lying on her front, bikini top unclipped. He was perturbed to see the Lebanese encamped on the other side of the pool playing bridge. There was a fat one, far fatter than Morgan, in a white shirt and Bermuda shorts. The others wore tiny swimming suits like jock straps: two thin weaselly men—one of whom had a face pitted like a peach stone—and the fourth, gratingly handsome in a lounge-lizard kind of way, with a thin moustache and a thick springy rug of hair over a lean and muscly chest. Morgan worried rather about him; he kept looking over at the girl.

There was a persistent roaring in his head; furious red static grumbled and flushed behind his eyes; slabs of heat burned his thighs and belly. Morgan was sunbathing. It was agony. He sat up, rockets and anti-aircraft shells pulsating and exploding everywhere he looked, and reached behind him for the bottle of beer he'd ordered and kept in the shade beneath a lounger. The bottle was still cool, the green glass slippy with beads of condensation. Morgan took great juddering pulls at it, beer spilling from the upended bottle over his chin, dripping onto his chest. His brain seemed to soar and cartwheel with the alcohol. He let out a silent, satisfying belch and stood up ready to plunge into the pool.

The first thing he noticed was the girl's striped towel, occupied only by the damp imprint of her body. Then he heard a ripple of laughter from the shallow end of the pool and he saw her chatting to the hairy Lebanese, who, as Morgan gazed, stood on his hands and walked round with his brown legs waving comically above the water, to the delighted laughter of the girl.

It can only have been this flirtatious display of agility, coupled with the dizzying effects of the cold beer, that drove Morgan to the diving board. As he climbed laboriously to the top he grew increasingly aware of the absurdity of the position he had committed himself to, and of all its hackneyed connotations. He sensed, as he emerged on the highest board, the attention of the others below turn to him. He had only seconds to decide. Beyond the lip of the board he saw the girl looking up at him, and the frank interest of her gaze inspired him and yet was somehow depressing. Depressing to think that he had stooped to these despised macho techniques to gain the girl's absorption, and inspiring to find that they actually worked. He hitched up the waistband of his trunks. He would compromise: he wouldn't dive— he wasn't sure if he could remember how—and he wouldn't climb back down. No, he would jump. He tried to saunter casually to the edge of the board. The pool slowly revealed itself beneath him. He thought: good God, it seems higher from up here. Bloody high. Shouldn't there be some kind of legal limit . . . ? His doubts were cut off in midstream as he realised with a gulp of horror that he had missed his step and clownishly fallen forward off the board, not an elegant vertical jump, but at a gradually diminishing angle of forty-five degrees to the water. And as the glinting, shimmering surface rushed up to meet him, Morgan spread his arms in a grotesque parody of a swallow-dive and belly-flopped full force with a ghastly echoing smack.

Everything was white. White and fizzing as if he were immersed in a glass of Andrews Liver Salts. He felt strong arms pulling him to the side. He felt his hands on the tiled edge of the pool. He took great gasping mouthfuls of air. His vision cleared. The hairy Lebanese was by his side, an arm protectively round his shoulders. Morgan shrugged him off and looked up. The stewardess crouched on the pool edge above him, concern filling her eyes.

"Are you all right?" she asked. "It made an awful sound."

"Mmmm. Sure," Morgan wheezed. "I'm . . . fine."

He rested in his room all afternoon. The entire front of his body was flushed and tingling for at least two hours. The girl had gathered up his stuff, draped a towel across his winded shoulders and led him back to his block. He felt as if he had just swum the Channel; his lungs heaved, his body creaked with pain and he could barely gasp replies to the girl's worried solicitations. And when the pain and the agony subsided it was replaced with an equally cruel shame. Morgan writhed with embarrassment on his bed, cursing his ridiculous pretensions, his preposterous life-guard conceit and his absurd gigolo rivalry.

He ate his evening meal as soon as the restaurant opened. Only the Americans accompanied him but they maintained a frosty indifference. He inquired at the desk if there had been any word about the coup or news of the airport opening. The reception clerk told him that there was nothing but martial music on the radio but he planned to listen to the BBC world service news at nine. Perhaps that would give them some reliable information.

Morgan found a dark corner of the bar and flicked through old magazines for a while. No one interrupted him. There was no sign of the stewardess or the Lebanese. He ordered a large whisky. To hell with everyone, he thought.

Shortly after nine Morgan went out to look for the receptionist but the desk was empty. He waited for a few minutes and then decided to turn in early. He was walking down the passageway that led out to his block when he heard noises coming from behind a door marked GAMES ROOM. He stopped. He could hear a man's voice, an indistinct seductive bass. He then heard some feminine giggles. He was about to walk on when he heard the girl say, "No. Stop it. Come on now." He listened again. She grew more insistent. "Look. *Stop* it. Really. Come on, it's your serve." She was still giggling but it seemed to Morgan that a worried tone had entered her voice. Then: *"Ow!*—Honestly, cut it out! No. Stop it, please."

Morgan pushed open the door. The girl stood there

in the hairy Lebanese's arms. He seemed to be biting
her shoulder. As Morgan entered they broke apart, and
the girl, blushing, quickly readjusted the strap of her
cream dress which had slipped down her arm. Morgan
felt supremely foolish for the second time that day. He
wasn't at all clear about what one was meant to say in
situations like this. The girl smiled; he felt slightly reassured. She seemed pleased to see him and backed away
from the Lebanese. He smiled, too, white and gold teeth
beneath his moustache.

"How you feel?" he asked Morgan confidently, tap-
ping his stomach. "The belly. Is good?"

They were standing in front of a Ping-Pong table.
Morgan walked over to it and picked up a bat. He
swished it menacingly about.

"My turn to serve, I think," he said pointedly, in as
clipped and cool a tone as he could summon. "Why don't
you push off, Abdul? Eh?"

The Lebanese looked at the girl, who earnestly studied her fingernails. He gave a snort of laughter and
pushed past Morgan out of the room, saying something harsh and guttural in Arabic, as if he had a forest
of fish bones stuck in his throat. An expressive language, Morgan admitted to himself, hugely relieved.

Morgan and the stewardess went to the bar and had
a quiet, mature laugh about it all. There had been no
real problem, the girl insisted. He was just getting a little fresh. Still, she was glad Morgan had walked in. They
had a few drinks. The stewardess said her name was
Jayne Darnley. She'd come down with a touch of upset
tummy and had to be left behind when the last plane
took off. Morgan bought some more drinks. She was
wearing a loose satin dress and Morgan admired the roll
of her heavy breasts beneath the bodice as she reached
down into her bag for a menthol cigarette. They got on

famously; Morgan even laughed about his ill-fated dive. "It was terribly brave of you," stated Jayne. She came, it transpired, from Tottenham and had worked on "promotions" before becoming a stewardess. The whisky made Morgan feel virile and capable; he could smell the pungent scent she used, and the click of the sentry's boots in the foyer lent a frisson of exotic danger to the atmosphere. He started to lie grandly. Yes, he admitted, he was leaving this country for a new posting: Paris. He was going to be defence attaché at the Paris embassy. "Ooh, Paree," enthused Jayne. "I *love* Paris." And from there, Morgan confided, a spot of work at the UN perhaps. After that, who knows? Although his first loyalty had always been to the service, he'd always had a secret yearning for the cut and thrust of political life, and with his experience, maybe. . . . Morgan went on to conjure up a large, interesting and cultured family, a trendy public school, a starred first. He created a modest private income, a chic *pied-à-terre* in Chelsea; he fabricated costly hobbies and recondite enthusiasms, and spoke knowingly of half-famous intellectuals, minor royalty, television-show compères. As the whisky and his rising sexual excitement fuelled his imagination, so Jayne grew more entranced, edging forward on her chair, lips set apart in a ready smile of anticipation. Her eyes gleamed; what a good time she was having. Morgan concurred, and called for another Pernod and blackcurrant.

At midnight, both a little unsteady on their feet, they walked arm in arm up the pathway towards the residential blocks. Crickets telephoned endlessly all around. The path bifurcated. "Well," Jayne sighed, raising her face to his, "I go this way."

Morgan was quite satisfied with their love-making. It hadn't exactly made the earth move for him but Jayne

had produced a flattering tocsin of appreciative yips and
mews as he had humped away in the dark heat of the
room. He lay back now, his chest and belly heaving, and
thought how perhaps events had not turned out so
badly.

Jayne smoked a cigarette and whispered compli-
ments to him. Then she propped herself on one elbow
and gazed down at his face, tracing its contours with a
sharp red fingernail.

"I can't believe my luck," she confided softly. "To . . .
well, to meet you like this." Her thin lips pecked at his
face like a dabbing fish. "I'd just never have thought it
possible. Someone like you. You know?"

Morgan wasn't sure that he did, and for the first time
he found the ambiguity somewhat unsettling.

Jayne still maintained the same vein of ingenuous lyri-
cism in the morning before she returned to her own
room. Strangely, and against his better judgement, she
elicited similar vague responses from Morgan. He was
half-asleep and unused to finding a warm naked woman
in his bed on waking up. The associated sensations of
comfort and cosy eroticism were agreeably complemen-
tary. They admitted that, yes, they both really liked
each other; and it was funny how people like them—
from such different backgrounds—got along so tre-
mendously easily. It was almost, almost like fate really,
wasn't it? What with her illness, his puncture and, of
course, the coup. Didn't he think so? Jayne prompted,
searching beneath the sheet. A squirming Morgan felt
bound to agree, suggesting, almost before he realised
what he was saying, that once this thing was over they
really ought to see some more of each other. Miracu-
lously, it seemed, Jayne had two weeks of leave coming
up and nothing in particular planned for them. If

Morgan had some time to spare before his Paris posting came through, it would be fun to see each other in
London. Of course, Morgan whispered, nuzzling her
neck, of course.

But then Jayne was out of bed and swiftly into her
cream dress, patting her face with powder and applying fresh lipstick. She kissed him on the cheek.

"See you downstairs," she said. "Let's go to the pool
again."

Alone, Morgan dressed slowly. Post-coital tristesse, not
an ailment he was usually afflicted with, weighed heavy
on him today. He moved like a man deep in thought,
like a hasty investor who's just had the dubious rami-
fications of his latest deal explained. His early swaggering confidence, his locker-room bravado, his smug
self-congratulation had mysteriously dissipated, leaving
a querulous, nagging tone of rebuke and stale second
thoughts.

He walked distractedly into the hotel lobby, his mind
preoccupied, and was surprised to find it full of the
guests, their luggage and the same flustered BOAC official who had met him at the airport gates two days
previously.

"Ah, Mr. Leafy," he said to Morgan. "Here at last.
You'll be glad to know that the airport has reopened,
diplomatic relations have been established, and you're
flying out on"—he consulted his clipboard—"the third
plane. Eleven forty-five this morning. We're getting you
all along to the airport as quickly as possible, as things
are a bit chaotic, to put it mildly. If you could report
back to me here in fifteen minutes?" He turned to answer a phone ringing on the reception desk.

Jayne came up to Morgan. She was wearing a lurid
print dress and large round sunglasses.

"We're on the same plane," she said. "Isn't that a

stroke of luck? Don't worry, I'll see we get sitting beside each other. I've a friend at the airport."

Morgan smiled wanly, muttered something about
having to pack, and returned to his room.

As he laid his clothes in his suitcase he felt unfamiliar symptoms of panic sweep over him, as if he were
some inefficient refugee too late to flee the advance of
an invading army. He felt like a crapulous sailor who's
overstayed his shore leave, watching his ship steam out
of harbour. Things were moving far too quickly, he realised; he no longer felt in control. Suddenly they were
leaving for home and he found himself teamed up with
this Jayne, thinking of themselves as a couple, without
really understanding how it had all come about. He felt
mystified, bemused. Who was this woman? Why was she
making assumptions about him, organising his life?

The minibus that was to take them to the airport contained only two of the Lebanese and Jayne, who had
kept Morgan a seat. As he settled in beside her, stu-
diously avoiding the hostile looks of the others, she
squeezed his hand and smiled at him. Morgan felt sick,
queasy, like a man on a tossing ship who realises he
should have refused those second helpings. God, he
hadn't envisaged anything like this at *all*, he reflected,
as Jayne explained about her friend at the airport. No,
by Christ, it was getting terribly out of hand. Why had
he lied so convincingly; as if he were short-listed for
foreign secretary? Why hadn't he been callous and
knowing, taken his pleasure like the chance acquaint-
ances they were? Then he felt foolish and sad as he
reasoned that it had only been the lies and false gran-
deur that had attracted the woman to him at all, and
that without the fake glitter and borrowed glory, Morgan Leafy was of little consequence as a person, a mi-

nor district official leaving for a boring desk job in central London; and that without the stories and the make-believe, he could have stared and lusted at the side of the pool or fantasised in the bar for days and she would probably never have noticed he was there.

The low prefab shacks of the airport building heaved and pulsed with hot, irate travellers like some immense festering yeast culture. Queues intertwined and doubled back on themselves before makeshift desks, where airline clerks mindlessly flipped through damp sheets of passenger manifests and ticket counterfoils in a futile attempt to match names to seats, and parties to destinations. Beyond customs control, gangs of green-suited porters hurled bags onto lorries, and starched, impassive military police forced everyone to hand over their local currency.

After a two-hour struggle, Morgan and Jayne arrived in the departure lounge, their clothes mussed and sticky with perspiration, clutching handfuls of official departure forms and exchange-control declarations to be filled out in triplicate. Normally the blatant inefficiency and wanton lack of automation fixed Morgan in a towering rage, but today he was merely sullen and leaden-hearted. Jayne had clung to his arm throughout the obstacle course of the check-in and, dashing his last faint hope, had successfully arranged with her friend behind the desk for the two of them to have adjacent seats.

As she went up to the bar, Morgan gazed blindly at the ancient photographs of long-out-of-commission aircraft and thought of the appalling chain of events the coup had unwittingly set in motion. He mentally compared his parents' semi-detached in Pinner, where he would be staying, with the Chelsea mews flat he had

described to Jayne in such detail. He anguishedly contrasted his menial job off Whitehall, in a grimy office
block, with the post of defence attaché at the Paris embassy. He sighed in frustration as he considered how
he had meekly accepted Jayne's invitation to meet her
Mum and Dad the following Sunday. It was pathetic.
He felt like weeping.

Jayne returned with two warm bottles of Fanta orange. "All they had," she explained. "Come on, dear,
move up. Make room for little me."

Dear! Morgan's spirit finally collapsed. He felt he
couldn't simply tell her to go away, as he himself had
so deliberately contrived to deceive her. Perhaps when
she found out the truth she'd reject him. But he looked
at the tight lips sucking on a straw, the shrewd eyes with
their delta of discreet lines, the coruscating talons grip-
ping the Fanta bottle, and he thought, no, Jayne was
running out of time, and there wasn't much hope of
that.

At eleven o'clock their plane was called and they as-
sembled at the departure-lounge door. None of the
airport buses was functioning and they had to walk
across the shimmering apron to the plane. Morgan
plodded across the hot tarmac, his eyes on the heels of
the couple in front of him. The sun beat down on his
exposed head, causing runnels of perspiration to drip
from his brow. Jayne's hand was latched firmly in the
crook of his elbow.

They paused at the foot of the steps. Morgan looked
up. Stewardesses beamed at the entrance to the plane.
He'd never trust those smiles again. He felt he was about
to climb the gallows. He looked at Jayne. Her eyes were
invisible behind the opaque lenses of her sunglasses. She
squeezed his arm and smiled, revealing patches of orange on her teeth that had smudged from her lips.

"Oh, look," she said, gesturing beyond Morgan's shoulder. "Must be someone important. Bet he tries to barge the queue.'"

Morgan turned and saw an olive-green Mercedes driving across the tarmac from the airport buildings at some speed. A pennant cracked above the radiator grille. The car stopped and a young man got out. He held a piece of paper in his hand. He was tall and sunburnt and wore a well-pressed white tropical suit similar to the one Morgan had on. He was like the Platonic incarnation of everything Morgan had tried to create in his conversations with Jayne. And for Jayne, he was the misty image, the vague ideal of the man she fancied she had met in the airport hotel. They both stared uncomfortably at him for a brief moment, then simultaneously turned away, for his presence made reality a little hard to bear.

The young man walked up the line of waiting passengers.

"Mr. Leafy?" he called in a surprisingly high, piping voice. "Is there a Mr. Morgan Leafy here?"

At first, absurdly, Morgan didn't react to the sound of his own name. What could this vision want with him? Then he put up his hand like a school-kid who's been asked to own up.

"Telex," the young man said, handing Morgan the piece of paper. "I'm from the embassy here," he added. "Frightfully sorry we didn't get to you before this. Hope it wasn't too bad in the hotel . . ." He went on, but Morgan was reading the telex.

"LEAFY," he read, "RETURN SOONEST NKONGSAMBA. YOU ARE URGENTLY REQD. RE LIAISING WITH NEW MILITARY GOVT. ALL CLEAR LONDON. CARTWRIGHT."

Cartwright was the High Commissioner at Nkongsamba. Morgan looked at the young man. He couldn't speak, his throat was choked with emotion. He handed the Telex to Jayne. She frowned with incomprehension.

"What does this mean?" she asked harshly, the poise cracking for an instant as Morgan stepped out of the queue.

"Duty calls, darling." There seemed to be waves crashing and surging behind his rib cage. He felt dazed, abstracted from events. He waved his hands about meaninglessly, like a demented conductor. "Absolutely nothing I can do." He had reached the Mercedes; the young man held the back door open for him. The embarking passengers looked on curiously. He saw the Americans. "Hey!" the woman shouted angrily, "you're British!" He suppressed a whoop of gleeful laughter. "Sorry, darling," he called again to Jayne, trying desperately to keep the elation from his voice. "I'll write soon. I'll explain everything." A final shrug of his shoulders and he ducked into the car. It was deliciously cool; the air-conditioning whirred softly.

"I'll come as far as the airport buildings," the young man said deferentially. "Then this'll take you straight back up the road to Nkongsamba if that's okay with you."

"Oh, that's fine," said Morgan, loosening his tie and waving to Jayne as the car moved off. "Oh, yes. That's absolutely fine."

Long Story Short

PART ONE

Louella and I stood alone in the darkening garden. There was the first hint of autumn frost in the evening. The soft light from the drawing-room windows set shimmers glowing in her thick auburn hair. Louella hugged herself, crushing her full breasts with her forearms. I felt an almost physical pain of love and desire in my gut.

"I think they're lovely," she said, turning to face the house.

"So do I . . . oh, you mean Ma and Pa?"

"Of course. I'm glad I've met them."

"They like you, too, you know, very much." I moved beside her and put my arm round her slim waist. I rested my forehead on hers. "I like you too," I said whimsically. She laughed, showing her pale throat, and we hugged each other. I stared past her at the trees and bushes slowly relinquishing their forms to the night. Then I felt her posture change slightly.

"Well, hello, little brother," came a deep, sardonic voice. "What have we got here?"

It was Gareth. And somehow I knew everything would be spoilt.

***

Actually it wasn't Gareth at all. It was Frank. God, I'm
tired of this relentless artifice. Let's start again, shall we?

PART TWO

Louella and William stood alone in the darkening garden. There was the first hint of autumn frost in the
evening. . . . drawing-room windows, yes, . . . crushing her full breasts, etc., . . . almost physical pain and
so on.

"I don't see why you're so upset," Louella said. "I
mean, he is your brother. If I'm going to be one of the
family I might as well meet him."

"But he's such a shit. A fat, smarmy shit and a mean
little sod to boot. I know you won't like him. He's just
not our type," William said petulantly, conscious of the
fact that he was only stimulating Louella's interest.

They heard the sound of a car in the drive. William
felt his throat tighten. Louella tried to appear noncha-
lant—with only partial success.

Frank opened the drawing-room windows and saun-
tered into the garden to join them. He was wearing a
maroon cord suit with unfashionably flared trousers and
a yellow nylon shirt. A heavy gold ingot swung at his
throat. His once-even features, William noticed, had
become thickened and distorted with fat. He was almost completely bald now.

No, it's no good. It keeps getting in the way, this
dreadful compulsion to tell lies. (You write fiction and
what are you doing? You're telling lies, pal, that's all.)
And besides, it's very unfair to Frank, who was very
good-looking, exceptionally well dressed and had as thick
and glossy a head of hair as Louella in Part One.
Louella—the real Louella—in fact had dyed blond hair,

but I've always had a hankering for auburn. (Come to that, she doesn't have full breasts either.)

To get rid of the fiction element, perhaps I should begin by distinguishing myself from the "I" in Part One. I—now—am the author (you know my name—check it out). The "I" in Part One is fictional, *not* me. Neither is the "William" in Part Two. It's just a device. No doubt, in any case, you thought to yourself, "hold on a second," as you read Part Two. "Little bit odd, this," you probably thought: "Character's got the same name as the author. Something fishy here." But you must watch out for that sort of thing; it's an error readers are prone to fall into. There are a lot of Williams about. Lots. It doesn't need to be me.

But now, having got rid of all this obfuscation, I am speaking to you directly. The author talking to the reader—whoever you are. Imagine me as a voice in your ear, unmediated by any notions or theories you may have heard about books and stories, textuality and reading, that sort of thing. I was, as it so happens, in actual fact, really engaged to a girl called Louella once, and I did have a brother called Frank. And certain factual events to do with the three of us inspired, were at the back of, the two beginnings I attempted. Louella was an American girl. I'd met her in New York, fallen in love, got engaged and had brought her back to England to meet my parents. She also met Frank.

Frank. Frank was the sort of older brother nobody needs. Tall, socially at ease, rich, good job (journalist on an up-market Sunday). Very attractive too. He had a polished superficial charm which, to my surprise, managed to take in one hell of a lot of people. But he was a smug, self-satisfied bastard and we never really liked each other. He always needed to feel superior to me.

"Pleased to meet you," Frank said to Louella, holding on to her hand far longer than William thought necessary.

"Hi," said Louella. "William's told me so much about you."

Frank laughed. "Listen," he said. "You don't want to believe anything he says."

He didn't say that, in fact. But it's typical of the sort of thing I can imagine him saying. Anyway, I only did that just to show you how easy it is—and how different. I can make Frank bald, add four inches to Louella's bust, supply William with a flat in Belgravia. But it's not going to solve anything. Because—to cut a long story short (quite a good title, yes?)—I really did love Louella (we'll still call her that, if you don't mind—saves possible embarrassment). I wanted to marry her. And that bastard Frank steadily and deliberately took her away from me.

At the time we were staying with my parents. We hadn't fixed a date for the wedding, as we were waiting until we had a house first. However, plans were being made; Louella's mother was going to fly over; a guest list was being drawn up. Frank was very subtle. He contented himself with being incredibly *nice*. He was around a lot and spent a great deal of time with Louella—just chatting. I was away in London (my parents live near Witney, Oxfordshire) trying to get a job. I can still remember—quite vividly—sitting on the London train, rigid with a kind of frustrated rage. I knew exactly what was happening. I could sense Louella's increasing fascination with Frank but there was nothing I could do about it, no accusation I could level, without being accused in turn of chronic paranoia. Nothing physical had happened between Louella and Frank, yet in a way she was more intimate with him than she'd ever been with me.

I couldn't stand it any longer. The house seemed to brim with their complicity. I felt pinioned by their innuendoes, webbed in by their covert glances. It was impossible. Yet the whole relationship was occurring at such a subliminal, cerebral level that any apportioning of blame on my part would look like an act of near insanity. So I went away. I said I had to be in London for an entire week job-hunting and having interviews. I entrusted Louella to my parents' care, but I knew Frank wouldn't be far away.

I took up an uncomfortable post in the wood behind my parents' house, armed with a pair of powerful binoculars, and watched the comings and goings. I saw Frank arrive the next day, homing in unerringly. Saw them walk in the garden, go out for drives. Saw Frank take my place at the family dinner table, pouring wine, recounting anecdotes that I should have been telling.

In fact, William hated Frank with all the energy he could summon. Hated his lean, permanently tanned face, his fake self-deprecating smile. Despised his short fingernails, his modishly scruffy clothes. Loathed his intimate knowledge of current affairs, his casual travelogues. And he ached when Louella touched his arm in admiring disbelief as Official Secrets were dropped, off-the-record confidences disclosed. Suffered when she showed her pale pulsing throat as she laughed at his smart in-jokes.

Sorry. Sorry. It's a lapse, I know. I promised. But fiction is so safe, so easy to hide behind. It won't happen again.

It was a Sunday afternoon when I became really alarmed. My vigil in the wood had lasted three days (sleeping in my car: extremely uncomfortable) and I was beginning to wonder if I'd overdramatised things rather.

Mother and Father had gone out on some interminable Sunday ramble in the car. (I sense that I haven't really done my parents justice—not that they're all that interesting really—but they play no significant part in the following events.) Then Frank came round in his car— a Triumph Stag: pure Frank, that. There was some activity in the house. Frank appeared briefly in the sitting room with two suitcases. I scampered through the garden and peered round the corner of the house. Frank was rearranging luggage in the boot. I saw him take out a fishing rod and repack it. Then Louella appeared. She seemed quite calm. She said, "Have you left a note for them?"

Frank: "Yes, on the hall table."

Louella: "What about William?"

Frank: "Oh, don't worry about him. Ma and Pa will break the news."

Reader, imagine how I felt.

They drove off. I knew where they were going. I went inside and read the note Frank had written to my parents. It went something like this.

> Louella and I have gone away for a few days. We have fallen very much in love and want to think things over. Please break this to William as gently as possible. Back sometime next week.
>
> Love, Frank.

The family have a small cottage on the west coast of Scotland. We have spent many summers there. I knew that was where Frank was heading. The fishing rod gave it away. Fly fishing is his great "passion." He thinks it somehow both intellectual—respectable literature on the sport—and gentlemanly: Alec Douglas Home and the

Queen Mother do it. I filled my car up with petrol and
went to London. There I dropped in on a few friends
and made some calls. Then, that night, I followed them
north.

The family cottage—more of a house to be honest—
lies off the main road near the village of A———.
(Funny how this is meant to make it more realistic. It
seems so obvious. Why not give the name. It's Achran-
ich, not far from Oban. I'm not interested in mislead-
ing you.) Behind the house is one of those typical
Scottish hills, khaki-green, shaded with brown and purple, covered in a thick, moss-sprung grass. An ener-
getic hike over this and you find one of the best stretches
of Highland salmon-river in Scotland. That was why
Frank brought his fishing rod. He can never resist it.

Picture the scene. Me, huddling chilled in a damp
clump of bracken, exhausted after an overnight drive.
Waiting for Frank to appear. And, sure enough, he does,
after a late breakfast. (Porridge, kippers, toast and
marmalade. That's just a guess. How could I know what
he'd had for breakfast?) He looks disgustingly pleased
with himself as he strides up the hill with his rod and
his bags and his tackle, passing—oh—within thirty yards
of my hiding place. I keep still. After all, I know where
he's going.

Thirty minutes later I catch up with him. He's at the
big pool. The river hurtles and elbows its way down the
hillside. It's the colour of unmilked tea and is shallow,
with a bed of rounded pebbles and stones. Except at
one point. Here there is a cascade that froths into a
large, deep, chill pool. A great angled slab of rock juts
out into the pool, setting up eddies and deflecting cur-
rents. Beneath this the fish lurk. Stand on the lip of the
cascade (thigh waders obligatory) leaning back against
the nudge and pressure of the water, cast down into the

pool below the rock and you can't go wrong. Frank was positioned exactly so. Two small creaming waves where his green rubber waders broke the solid parabola of the falling water.

I enter the stream twenty yards above the slosh down. Frank can't hear me because of the noise of the falling water. I stand behind him. I tap his shoulder. He looks round. His eyes widen in wordless surprise. He instinctively jerks back as though expecting a blow. It is enough. He loses his balance and, with a despairing, grabbing whirl of arms, is flipped over the edge into the pool. I don't even wait to see what happens. Waders filled with water, heavy clothes sodden, freezing water. He'd go down like . . . like a stone.

I was in London by late evening. I was summoned home by a phone call just before lunch the next day. Dreadful news. I have to take the twin blows of my fiancée's infidelity and my brother's accidental death. My parents are grim and unforgiving; they think Louella is in some way responsible. I am shocked and stunned. But poor Louella. She has to turn somewhere. I am deeply hurt, but relent under the shared burden of grief. We go for drives and talk and, to cut a long story short, we . . .

But I've lost you, haven't I? Where was it? That bit about me hiding in the wood? Or setting up my alibi and following them to Scotland? It wasn't a question of continuing to suspend disbelief, but rather the belief beginning to crumble away of its own accord. You were saying: "If he wants us to believe him; if he wants us to think we're reading something true, then surely confessing to a murder in cold print is, well, a bit implausible?"

You're right, of course. I got carried away. Fiction took

over once again. Anyway, I could never do a thing like that, could I?

P.S.: Frank and "Louella," wherever you are, if you should happen to read this—no hard feelings? It's just a joke.

ARMADILLO

The life of Lorimer Black, insurance adjustor, is about to be turned upside down. The elements at play: a beautiful actress with whom he is falling in love; an odd associate whose hiring, firing, and rehiring make little sense; a rock musician whose loss—in this case of his mind—may be "adjusted" by the insurance company. Black uncovers a web of fraud involving virtually everyone he knows, and in which he becomes increasingly entangled.

Fiction/Literature/0-375-70216-4

AN ICE-CREAM WAR

William Boyd brilliantly evokes the private dramas of a generation swept up by the winds of war. As the sons of the world match wits and weapons, desperation makes bedfellows of enemies—and traitors of friends and family. *An Ice-Cream War* deftly renders lives capsized by violence, chance, and the irrepressible human capacity for love.

Fiction/Literature/0-375-70502-3

THE BLUE AFTERNOON

Sprawling across three continents and two eras, this atmospheric novel opens in Los Angeles in 1936, when architect Kay Fischer is approached by an elderly man named Salvador Carriscant, who claims to be her father—and who insists she accompany him to Lisbon in search of the great lost love of his life.

Winner of the Los Angeles Times *Book Prize in Fiction*
Fiction/Literature/0-679-77260-X

THE DESTINY OF NATHALIE X

A tourist stranded in the Dordogne valley in the 1920s finds a French countess waiting amorously in his hotel room. A widowed Englishwoman and a Portuguese poet meet every Christmas in 1930s Lisbon to share an erotic delirium before parting for another year. These and nine more stories chart the euphoria of love, the anguish of loss, and the gnawings of ambition.

Fiction/Short Stories/0-679-76784-3

VINTAGE INTERNATIONAL
Available at your local bookstore, or call toll-free to order:
1-800-793-2665 (credit cards only).